Run, Little Bunny

A High Five Novella
Book #4

By Serena Pier

Overgrown frat antics can be endearing. Chad Braun wants to show you that.

Reading Order

High Five Novella Series:

Part 1

Santa's Coming

Cupid's Shot

Shamrock Kisses

Part 2

Run, Little Bunny

Falling For Red
Releasing June 5th, 2025

1

Anna

Saturday, April 19th

"How many eggs are you going to get?" I ask my nephew Cam, who's squirming in his car seat, growing tired of the straps.

"All of them!" he shouts, bubbling with excitement for the annual Easter egg hunt in our town of Lake Geneva, Wisconsin. I lean over, adjusting his straps a little to make him more comfortable.

"Some of the eggs have special prizes," I remind him. "You could win a new bicycle or even gift cards."

"I want candy!"

My sister Megan and I make eye contact through the rearview mirror, both smiling at his four-year-old honesty.

I can't wait to have kids. My friends think I'm crazy since I'm only twenty-two, but I've always wanted to be a mom. Seeing all the families in the park as we approach, it makes the feeling stronger. Opening my period tracking app, I chuckle. *Ovulating.*

1

"What's so funny?" Megan asks as she pulls into the park's parking lot.

I hesitate, then shrug.

"Something deep is on your mind. Spill."

"Just thinking about the lack of options in this town."

"So, your date last night didn't go well?"

"Understatement. I spent three hours listening to him talk about crypto. I don't even know what Ethereum is, but apparently, I should care."

Megan snorts before we both get out of the car. I immediately spot the cutest couple in town, Emily Brown and Nicholas O'Malley. Emily's son skips in front of them, swinging his basket.

That's what I want. I want someone who loves these cheesy holiday traditions as much as I do. Nicholas is also a zaddy—a hot, older man—and I wouldn't be mad about that either.

"He's going to propose," Megan whispers as she lets Cam out of his car seat.

"What?! Already?"

"I heard he was in the jewelry store last week asking some very specific questions."

"He should know better ..." I laugh, even though I kind of love the small-town gossip mill. "For real? They haven't even been together for six months."

Still, I find it romantic.

Cam spots the colorful eggs scattered across the park's grass and takes off.

"Slow down!" Megan and I yell in unison, and then we smile at each other. I've been helping out more than usual since her husband was deployed, and I love being a bigger part of their lives.

"The basket!" I blurt out, realizing we left it in the trunk. "I'll get it."

Megan gives me a grateful smile, jogging after Cam while I head back to the car.

With Cam's personalized basket in hand, I chuckle at the sight of a giant Easter Bunny waving to everyone at the entrance. The costume is ridiculous with a green vest, blue tuxedo jacket, huge fluffy head, and large glassy eyes.

That bunny has to be over six feet tall.

The Easter Bunny raises his hand like he's asking for a high-five. I smile awkwardly and slap his giant paw. "Anna!" a voice calls out from behind the mask as our hands meet.

I freeze. Okay, this is creepy. How does he know my name? I can't quite figure out who's behind the costume, and I'm too embarrassed to stand around and ask. Raising the basket as a kind of excuse, I continue toward Cam and my sister.

Kids are nearly salivating at the thousands of pastel-colored eggs scattered across the grass.

"Does the Easter Bunny keep looking at me?" I ask Megan as we walk farther into the park, trying to sound casual, though my heart's racing a little.

She glances over, raising an eyebrow. "No, don't be ridiculous. He's probably scanning the crowd. There's a ton of people here."

"It feels like it."

Megan shrugs, but I can't shake the feeling. Every time I glance back, the bunny's giant eyes seem locked on me, like he's watching my every move.

"Maybe he thinks you're cute," Megan teases, nudging me with her elbow.

Cam tugs at my jacket, pulling me out of my thoughts. "What's your favorite color?" he asks.

"Orange."

"I'll grab an orange egg for you." His little face lights up, and I pull him in for a side hug. He's the cutest, and moments like this remind me of why I want my own family someday.

A woman's voice crackles through the speakers, explaining the rules for the egg hunt. Thankfully, Cam's age group is up first.

"Did you listen?" Megan asks him. "You can only grab ten eggs."

"Ten eggs," Cam repeats, looking out at the plastic eggs in front of him, ready to run.

The air horn blares, and dozens of kids dash across the field. I watch the adorable chaos unfold but can't shake the feeling that someone's watching me.

"Seriously," I whisper to Megan, glancing back at the Easter Bunny. "He's definitely looking at me."

She gives me a skeptical look. "Okay, now you're being paranoid."

Maybe she's right. Maybe I'm imagining things.

But as the kids scramble for eggs and parents cheer them on, I steal one more glance over my shoulder—and sure enough, those giant bunny eyes are locked on me.

2

Chad

I've done some embarrassing things in my life—drunken karaoke ballads, ridiculous dares—but nothing, *nothing*, compares to standing here in this godforsaken Easter Bunny costume. All because I lost my fantasy football league. Three hours of fucking torture playing Buttons the Bunny at Lake Geneva's annual Easter egg hunt while my so-called friends laugh their asses off from a safe distance.

Seriously, I'm thirty-four years old. You'd think we'd be past this kind of nonsense by now, but clearly, we are not. The worst part is, deep down, I know none of us are growing up anytime soon. Not with stunts like this still on the table.

I shift in the bunny costume, my white parachute pants rustling awkwardly. The costume is somehow making me sweat even though it's barely fifty degrees. At least the mask hides my face. Buttons the Bunny's expression is frozen in a permanent state of wide-eyed horror, which suits me just fine at this point.

As if the universe has a sick sense of humor, I spot her. *Anna.* Great.

Anna started working at La Nonna about a year ago, and ever since, I've practically made it my second home. I tell myself it's because of the food, but honestly, it's mostly because of her. She's hilarious, quick-witted enough to keep me on my toes, and always wearing something that clings to her hourglass figure. Anna's a classic beauty—long blonde hair, blue eyes. Why does she have to be so damn cute?

She's way too young for me. Younger than my youngest sister. I try not to think about the age gap, but standing here in this stupid bunny suit isn't exactly helping my case. I mean, what kind of grown man does this to himself?

I raise my hand to wave at her as she walks past. It seems like she's going to ignore me. But then she looks right at me and, to my surprise, she high-fives the giant paw.

"Anna!" I say through the mask, my voice muffled by the layers of faux fur. She blinks up at me, looking a little scared, before walking off toward the egg hunt. Can't blame her. If some random bunny said my name, I'd be creeped out too.

I watch her go. These jeans today, hugging her in all the right places. I sigh, replaying that interaction, coming up with a hundred ways it could've gone better.

Twenty-two. Too young. But everything about her draws me in. Outside of her looks, she's genuinely fun to talk to. Either way, I've been hanging around La Nonna more often than I'd care to admit.

"Chad!"

I turn toward the voice and spot my handler for the day—my buddy's wife, Lauren, who works for the park's district. She's all business, clipboard in hand, knitted eyebrows saying she's had about enough of this chaos.

"It's almost time for pictures with the kids," she says, tapping her watch. "Get over to the photo booth."

"Lucky me," I mutter under my breath, but I shuffle in her direction anyway. At least the photo booth means I don't have to do much except stand there and wave. The mask does all the smiling for me.

I get into position by the booth, and the photographer takes a test picture then shows it to me. The white gloves, shoe covers, and oversized bunny head make me look like something out of a nightmare. Kids are definitely going to cry being forced to take a photo with me.

This torture is almost over. There is beer in my future, I remind myself. Nicholas, the newest member of our fantasy league and owner of the bar High Five, is buying the first round of beers after this as a way to conclude our fantasy season.

Lauren gives me a thumbs up as she prepares to herd the first batch of sugar-fueled kids my way.

My eyes wander back to Anna. I wonder if she'll end up at High Five later. I know she enjoys going there sometimes. To be honest, I wouldn't mind seeing her in a setting outside of her work and when I'm not dressed like a cartoon character. Or maybe I should get over myself and ask her out next time I'm at La Nonna.

A kid runs up to me, and I bend down to give him a high-five. He laughs like it's the funniest thing ever. At least someone's enjoying this.

One more hour. I need to survive one more hour in this stupid suit, and then I can retire Buttons the Bunny for good.

3

Anna

"Time to take your photo with the Easter Bunny," my sister says to Cam, who's sitting in the grass, happily sorting through the contents of his Easter eggs. She turns to me with a mischievous look on her face. "You should get one too."

"Yeah, right! For all I know, there's some creepy old man under there."

She raises an eyebrow. "You're the one saying there are no options in this town, and you think this guy is into you, so go flirt with him."

"The Easter Bunny?"

"He can't be that creepy if the park district is letting him take photos with hundreds of kids."

"You want me to flirt with the Easter Bunny?"

"Not the Easter Bunny." She nudges me. "The guy behind the costume."

"Mmm ..."

Megan gives me her classic older sister dare face. "Take a photo with him. It'll make me smile for the rest of the day."

I sigh dramatically, but I can't resist. I'm not one to turn down a dare. Grabbing Cam's hand, the three of us head toward the line. As we wait, I find myself staring at the Easter Bunny. Who could be behind that fluffy mask? He's tall—like, really tall—and after seeing that lady from the park's district giggle with him, I'm starting to wonder if he's someone around her age. Maybe a friend of hers? He knows who I am, so he must live around here. Could he be one of my regulars at La Nonna?

A sudden thought strikes me, and I smirk. It's ridiculous, but ... "Have I ever told you about one of my regulars, Chad?" I ask Megan.

She squints. "The guy that owns the boat rental company?"

"Yeah."

"What about him?"

"I was thinking—what if he's the bunny?"

"Seems random, but ... his company is one of the sponsors of this event."

What if Chad is the bunny? "He's cute, but he's always given off big brother vibes."

Cute is a little bit of an understatement. He's just over six feet tall with light brown hair and brown eyes.

"He's also too old for you," she immediately chimes in.

"How do you know how old he is?"

"Because I'm a nosy lady that eats up all the gossip in this town." We both laugh at its truth. "Twelve years is a huge age gap ... especially at your age."

"Why are you trying to make me feel like a baby?"

"Because you're my baby sister."

"Just because I'm six years younger than you doesn't make me a baby."

"Says the baby."

I nudge her. "Well ... Chad's never said anything that would make me think he's interested."

Not that I've been looking for an in. I've been obsessed with Aaron Olson, the hottest guy in Lake Geneva, for the last year. But Aaron's off the market now ... and definitely not interested in me.

Chad. Replaying some of my conversations with him, I smile. He's funny and smart. He gave me some great advice when I was buying my car. Nothing but big brother vibes.

"Go ask Nicholas who the bunny is if you're so curious. He would know being on the town's business council and helping put on these events."

"I'm not that curious! I'm channeling my inner Nancy Drew."

"You're curious!"

But Chad's never outright flirted with me. Sure, he tips well, but nothing like the guys who use it as a form of flirting. The bunny, though ... the bunny's been unusually interested in me today.

"If you do my nails, I'll flirt with the bunny," I propose.

"Flirt how?"

"I'll give him a kiss on the cheek for the photo."

Megan gasps, her face lighting up. "You would not!"

"If you promise to do my nails, I will."

She cocks her head. "What if the bunny wants your number after?"

I burst out laughing. "Yeah, right."

"If the bunny is that obsessed with you, he'll ask for your number."

I roll my eyes. "We're not going to run every possible scenario while we wait in this line. I'm just going to give him a kiss on the cheek."

4

Chad

Standing in this oversized bunny suit, I've reached the point where my only goal is survival. The sun's beating down now, and the inside of this costume feels like a sauna. The mask blocks out most of my peripheral vision, so all I can do is wave at the blur of kids approaching for a photo. Each high-five feels like I'm clinging to my last shred of dignity.

It's almost over. I'll soon be retired as Buttons the Bunny for good. Then, beers. A lot of beers.

I sit on the hay bale, tired of standing, but I really don't want kids to sit on my lap for photos. That's weird, so I stand back up for more awkward crouching and kids crying at the sight of my freakishly large eyes.

There she is—Anna. Of course.

She's standing in line with her nephew and sister. I can't tell if it's the sweat or the fact that I've been harboring this crush on her for months, but my heart starts to race. I watch as they inch closer, and Anna's laughing at something Megan said. She looks too good in this cropped jacket and jeans. I usually see her in some variation of a black dress or black top and skirt. Always tight. *Another reason why I like going to La Nonna.*

And then Megan nudges her, and Anna looks at me—well, at Buttons the Bunny—with this cute face that looks like it's plotting something.

Interesting.

The line moves up, and Cam's there, bouncing in place as he steps up for his photo. I bend down, giving him a high-five and a wave, trying not to think about Anna standing a few feet away until the camera flashes.

I can't help it, though. My eyes keep drifting to her.

"Go on," Megan says, nudging Anna toward me. She approaches, her smile wide and teasing.

She's getting a photo? Cam goes back to his mom, and now it's me and Anna.

"You ready for this?" she asks, glancing at me—or the bunny, whatever—as if she's daring me to react. I try to act cool, giving her a little wave with my massive paw.

Before I can even process what's happening, Anna leans in, planting a kiss right on the side of the bunny's cheek.

She's fun.

I force myself to stay in character, waving to the camera as the photographer snaps a photo.

The moment feels like it lasts forever, and when Anna pulls back, she's still smiling. I swear there's something in her eyes—something teasing. She can't know it's me, right? But before I can figure it out, she's already stepping back to rejoin her family.

"Nice bunny," Megan says with a smirk as they walk away, and I stand there, frozen in the costume, feeling both ridiculous and … hopeful? I don't even know anymore.

As soon as they're out of sight, my phone buzzes in my

pocket—because yes, this bunny costume has pockets. It's a text from Nicholas.

> **NICHOLAS O'MALLEY**
>
> CB, you're killing it out there.
>
> Still up for beers at High Five after? We're daring you to keep the bunny suit on.

I groan. Of course the guys are.

> **CHAD BRAUN**
>
> You're kidding, right?

> **NICHOLAS O'MALLEY**
>
> Nope. It'll be legendary. Plus, you'll drink for free. You in?

I sigh and look down at the fluffy, white suit that's been torturing me for hours, then look around the crowd, trying to spot Anna. An idea strikes me. She doesn't know it's me. Or maybe she does, but either way, I can't let this day end without at least trying to make a move. If I'm going to embarrass myself further, I might as well go all the way.

Waving Lauren over, I ask her for a scrap of paper and a pen. She cocks a brow, but I'm not going to tell her why. I take off my oversized paws and scribble a note. *My handwriting is terrible.*

"You, me, High Five, one hour. I'll be the guy in the bunny suit." - Buttons the Bunny

I'll have enough time to run back to my place and shower. I need it after sweating in this suit. My hands are shaking a little as I fold it up. *What am I doing?* I shouldn't be this nervous. This is either going to be the dumbest idea I've ever had or a great one.

Spotting Anna again, she's standing near the park exit, talking with her sister. Now's my chance.

I shuffle over, the ridiculous parachute pants rustling as I go. Anna turns her head, I'm sure hearing the noise and wondering why the Easter Bunny is approaching. *Should I say something?* I extend my hand and the note and decide not to speak.

She looks at me, surprised, before glancing down at the folded paper. Then she smiles, taking the paper from my paw. I wave because what else can I do? She gives me a small wave as I retreat back to the photo booth, unsure where else to go until she leaves.

Will she show up? It's a crazy request to meet up with Buttons the Bunny at a bar.

5

Anna

"I told you the Easter Bunny was staring at me!" I squeal after reading the note and handing it to my sister.

She chuckles, reading it. "So, are you going to go to High Five?"

"Um ..."

"Oh, come on! This is what being young is all about. This is a story you're going to want to tell your kids someday."

"How I went on a date with the Easter Bunny?"

"I think very few people can say that ... probably the best thing ever for two truths and a lie."

"I mean, I was planning on spending today finishing an unhinged dark romance book I'm about a hundred pages into or ... I guess meeting Buttons the Bunny. Which is an equally unhinged activity."

"Real life is more interesting than those books."

Who's to say? I laugh inwardly.

"And I doubt the bunny is going to talk to you about crypto like the guy from last night."

"I hope not ... bet. I'm going to get a drink with Buttons."

6

Chad

In High Five's parking lot, I stare at the bunny mask in my passenger seat while drumming my fingers on the steering wheel. *Should I put it back on?* I mean, this is a story. This is raising the bar for next year's fantasy football antics. The rest of the costume is at home, smelling terrible on my patio. There was no way I was putting that back on. I chuckle, thinking about how when I have my own kids, there will be so many silly holiday traditions in my future. *I should keep the bunny suit.* That would be fun.

Am I really going to flirt with Anna Clark while wearing a bunny mask? There's a little safety in Anna not knowing it's me yet. Part of me wonders if she'd recognize me without the mask—like, by my body in a t-shirt and jeans. *Calm down, ego.* But the longer I sit here, the more I think. Maybe keeping the mask on is the smarter play. If she's not interested, she's none the wiser it's me. If she is ... well, then I guess she'll learn who I really am.

Stepping into the bar with the bunny mask on, Aaron Olson, the manager and main bartender, greets me with laughter.

"Chad! CB! Oh man, I'm dying right now. Never been happier to have turned down your fantasy league invite."

"It's Buttons today," I correct, examining Nicholas's recent renovations. He kept the dive bar charm intact—the worn, wooden beams and exposed brick give it that old-time feel, like you're stepping into a local pub that's been around forever. High Five is the kind of bar where you feel at home whether you're in for a quick drink or staying until closing.

"Buttons?" he repeats skeptically. "I thought you only had to wear that at the Easter egg hunt."

"Well, I was talked into keeping it going."

"Dude, how're you gonna drink with that thing on?"

"I'll have to use a straw."

"You're going to drink *beer* ... with a straw?"

"It looks like you're going to have to make me one of your fancy cocktails."

Aaron reaches for bottles, mixing something up while I watch. I'm feeling a bit ridiculous sitting here in half a bunny costume but also kinda loving the absurdity of it all.

He drops a straw into a bright, colorful cocktail, and I lift it in his direction. "The bar looks damn good. You and Nicholas kept the vibe."

Aaron leans onto the bar. "Yeah, we didn't wanna change too much. The place already had history, you know? It needed a little love before busy season."

Busy season. It's almost here, basically a month away. I'm about to have no free time. All the boats come out of storage next week. My mind begins to think about work. I slip the straw under my mask and take a long sip.

Looking around at the place, the renovations are perfect. "Still feels like the bar we all grew up in." I take another sip. "Also, I'm serious—you gotta call me Buttons today. I kinda have this thing going and a girl might be coming in to meet up with Buttons."

"Who?" Aaron arches a brow.

"Anna Clark."

"Anna?"

Nodding, I sip my drink. "I've been eating at La Nonna so much ... she's sweet."

Aaron smirks a little. "She could use a good guy ..."

"I'm feeling too old for her," I admit, drumming the side of my glass. "Part of the reason I'm keeping the mask on. I've always kept it casual, but ... I want to test the waters a bit. See what happens when it's not all about ordering pasta."

Aaron pulls one of my bunny ears. "Well, good luck, Buttons."

7

Anna

Why am I nervous to walk into High Five? I come in here after work most days for a drink. *Buttons.* This is so stupid; I can't believe the Easter Bunny is going to buy me a drink. Or that I'm actually excited about it.

Inside the bar, the first person I spot is Aaron Olson. Of course, he's working today. I flash him a friendly smile before I spot the back of the bunny mask on a guy in a t-shirt and jeans. He changed. So, the tall guy under the costume is in good shape. *Plot twist.* I laugh to myself, relieved it's not some old man. No tattoos. If only he had arm tattoos, that would be a dead giveaway. But still ... who is this?

"Hi," I say, feeling a little unnerved talking to a guy in a bunny mask.

"I'm surprised you came."

"Me too."

"What can I get you to drink, Anna?" Aaron asks.

I glance at the cocktail the bunny is drinking. "Whatever that is."

Why does Aaron have to have a front-row seat to this?

Me and the Easter Bunny. This is ridiculous, but what else can I do but lean into it?

"Ready for your busy day tomorrow?"

The deep, sexy, amused sound from behind the mask catches me off guard. *I've heard that voice before.*

"I'm not committing to the bit *this* much," he says as Aaron slides my drink over.

"Cheers, little bunny," he teases.

"Little bunny?"

He chuckles, and something about that laugh clicks in my mind. I'm pretty sure it's Chad. I bite my lip, choosing not to guess aloud just yet. "Why are you calling me little bunny?"

The big, creepy eyes of the mask tilt slightly downward. *Is he checking me out?*

"You're a little bunny compared to me."

"I thought you weren't committing to the bit?"

He laughs again. "What are your plans for tomorrow?"

"Brunch at my sister's with the whole family."

"Is that a good thing?"

"Yes! My family's great, and we always have fun together."

He props his chin on his hand, the bunny mask resting in it.

"What?" I ask, feeling a little self-conscious.

"You're very cute."

"You're kinda creepy looking."

"The mask is creepy. I know ... but I like that you're having fun with this."

"You're lucky I'm a curious person. So, give me a hint about who you are."

"No."

"No?" I repeat, realizing the tone is flirty. *I'm flirting*

21

with a guy in a bunny mask. I shake my head, amused by this situation. "Come on, please."

He wags the bunny head back and forth in an exaggerated manner. "I'm a foodie."

I roll my eyes. "Aren't we all? That's barely a hint."

"Why are you so curious about who I am?"

"I'm trying to rule out that you're not a serial killer."

He laughs heartily. *Definitely Chad*, I think. *Chad Braun*. I'm not mad about it. He's fun. I love when he comes into the restaurant. Checking out his arms ... I'm pretty confident it's Chad.

"Do you have any other little bunnies?" I ask, wanting to solve this mystery.

The bunny mask tilts again. "Rabbits? No."

Witty. I laugh way too much at him saying he doesn't have kids and take a sip of my drink. "I mean ... are you single?"

"Too single."

"Too single?" I repeat, raising an eyebrow.

"What about you?"

"Same. Too single. So, why are you in this mask?"

"I lost my fantasy league."

"I think you're having too much fun with the punishment."

"Maybe."

It's so weird not seeing his face, relying on tone alone to gauge his reactions.

"Aaron," I call out. "Should I be scared of this guy?"

Aaron looks up from behind the bar. "No."

Because this is all so ridiculous, I blurt out, "Should I go home with the bunny?"

There is a choking sound behind the bunny mask, and

Aaron's eyes dart between the bunny and me. "That's really a personal decision."

I groan. *Aaron is way too much of a gentleman.*

"Why are you trying to make me nervous?" the voice behind the mask asks.

"Nervous?"

"You're thinking about taking me home."

"No, I'm not!" I protest, though my face feels warm.

"Then why'd you ask?"

I shrug, taking another sip. *What if this isn't Chad?*

"Is this bunny bothering you?" Nicholas's voice interrupts, and I turn to see him smirking, standing with another guy in his mid- to late-thirties.

"No, he's nice."

Nicholas and the bunny fist bump. Then the other guy claps the bunny on the shoulder before they head to a high-top table. *Another clue.* The bunny is probably in his thirties. Chad is also in his thirties.

"Want to join your friends?" I ask.

"No."

"Why not?"

"You're more interesting."

8

Chad

Staring at her, I wonder if she suspects something about me. She's too comfortable in this situation. If the roles were reversed, I doubt I'd feel the same.

"Can I see your hand?"

"Why?" She arches a brow, suspicious but intrigued.

"I want to show you one of my bar tricks."

She smirks but extends her hand. I take it, palm-up. "Just as I thought," I say, teasing, as I examine the lines.

"What?" She leans in, curious now.

"You've got high standards for relationships."

"What?!" she nearly squeals.

I trace her love line slowly. "It starts under your index finger. That's not so common."

"Wait, you read palms?"

"I have sisters."

Her hand is soft, smaller than I expected. I trace more lines, but my fingers keep returning to the love line. "These branches here ... they mean you're both passionate and reasonable. That's very attractive."

"So, I'm not crazy?"

"Time will tell." She swats my arm. "It means you have a big heart."

Anna narrows her eyes playfully. "You really trust this 'science'?"

"I like that it gave me an excuse to hold your hand."

From the smile on her face, I know it landed.

"You have sisters?" she asks, glancing at me over the mask. I'm still holding her hand. She hasn't pulled it away, and I decide to keep tracing the lines on her palm.

"Three of them. I'm the oldest."

"Oldest and youngest ..."

"What do you mean?"

"I hear that's a good match," she says with a sly smile.

I smirk. Although I know her sister is older, I ask. "You're the baby?"

"The youngest. Not the baby."

"You don't like to be called baby?"

"The context is important for that word."

Anna is funny. I've always thought so. And I can't believe she hasn't pulled her hand back yet. I can feel the warmth of her skin against mine. It's nice.

"Let me show you one of my bar tricks." She pulls her hand back. "Aaron, can I have a bottle of beer?"

"Which one?"

"Any one."

He cocks a brow, then bends down to open a cooler before handing her a beer. She takes it and smiles at me before opening it with her teeth.

"Anna!" I yell with concern behind the mask. "Don't fuck up your teeth ... but that was impressive."

"Why don't you want me to fuck up my teeth?"

"Because you have a pretty smile."

"You have a creepy one."

"I know this mask is better suited for Halloween." We both laugh. "Alright, little bunny, do you want another drink? You don't have to drink the beer if you don't want to."

9

Anna

L ittle bunny. It's cute. I like that he's calling me that.
"First," I start, feeling flirty, "I need to know ... are you a *stan?*"

"Stan?"

He doesn't know the word. More proof he's older. *And maybe Chad Braun.* "Like, are you obsessed with me in a cute way ... before today?" I can't believe I phrased it like that. My cheeks flush.

"If the answer is yes, does that make me a stan?" he asks, and I nod, biting my lip. "I guess I'm an Anna Clark stan then."

I'm tempted to ask his real name, but I'm having too much fun with all of this to ruin the mystery. "You can buy me another one of these cocktails."

"Same as last time?"

"Yeah."

He calls over to Aaron. "Another cocktail for the little bunny and me."

"You really like calling me that."

"I think it's perfect for you." *I don't disagree.* "Claire,"

27

he says, getting the red-headed server's attention. "Can you tell Nicholas and Chris this beer is from us?"

Their server, who's also got to be in her thirties, takes the beer from his hand. I wish I would have gotten more of a hint there. I can't tell whether she knows him or not.

"Not a beer guy?" I ask, because Chad is definitely a beer guy.

"I'm a beer guy, but it would be too hard to drink with this mask on."

I smirk, then lean in slightly. "So, why are you *too* single?"

"Why are you?"

The lack of options around here ... but maybe I haven't been paying attention to the options.

"It's not fair that you can see me blushing and smiling, and I have no idea what's going on under there." I wave my hand in a circle at the bunny mask.

"Life isn't fair," he says, poking my side, making me giggle. I twist a strand of hair around my finger, thinking about how much I like it when he touches me.

"What are you thinking about?"

"How much I'm hoping you're one of my regulars at La Nonna."

The bunny is quiet for a beat before responding, "Time will tell."

"How much time?" I ask, leaning in closer, my curiosity getting the best of me.

"I haven't decided yet."

"When are you going to decide?" My heart races a little. The anticipation is killing me.

"When I know you're interested in more than this bunny mask."

"I'm *not* interested in the bunny mask!"

"You sure?"

"I'm *not* a furry!"

He bursts into laughter. "How do you even know what that means?"

"The internet." I shrug.

Just then, Aaron slides our drinks across the bar, and the bunny reaches for his. "Cheers to our half-blind date."

I tap my glass against his with a huge smile. Despite the mystery, the banter, and the weirdness, this whole thing is fun. *Way* more fun than the dark romance read ... and the date I went on last night.

"When are you taking me out on a real date?" Whoever he is, I want to know the real him.

10

Chad

"Aren't you demanding," I manage, while my mind races. I'm going to have to reveal myself soon. *Not here.* I think it should be on a proper date. "Do you want to go out with Buttons?"

"I hope to never see Buttons' crazy eyes ever again."

I'm relieved she's as over that persona as I am. "Alright. So, do you want to go to a nice dinner, or would you rather do some kind of activity?"

She tilts her head, thinking. "Why can't we do both?"

"That would be a really long first date." I smirk. "What if we hate each other an hour in?"

"You think you're going to want to bail?"

"No."

"You think I'm going to want to bail?"

I shrug, and she sips her drink. Everything about her body language says she's amused.

"Okay. We'll do both," I relent but am also excited to spend so much time with her. "When are you free this week?"

Anna's fingers slide across her lips, like she's suddenly shy. "Now you're nervous?"

"A little," she whispers, then takes another sip, avoiding looking at the bunny mask.

I reach out and grab her hand, playing with her fingers. "I'd really like to take you out."

"Tuesday."

My smile behind this mask is so big. Sliding my phone out of my pocket, I hand it to her. "Put your number in here so I can tell you where to meet me."

"You're not picking me up?" She raises an eyebrow.

"You're really eager to be trapped with me, huh?"

She chuckles, grabbing my phone. "I want you to pick me up."

"I'll pick you up, then. Where do you live?"

"Lake View Apartments."

"When I was your age, I lived there," I tell her, amused by the coincidence, and I think about how my buddy Jake now owns the building.

Her eyes light up as she bites her lip, clearly pleased with this new detail. "So, how old are you?"

"I'll tell you on Tuesday."

"Are you under forty?" She arches a brow, not letting me off the hook so easily.

"Are you used to getting everything you want?"

"I am the baby."

"I thought you didn't like that word."

"I told you. Context."

Fuck it. I yank her barstool closer to mine, closing the space between us, and lean in. "I want to give you everything you want."

11

Anna

Holy shit. "Okay, Buttons," I tease, trying to play it cool, but I'm freaked out by how turned on I am right now.

"Okay, little bunny," he growls in response, his voice low and rough.

"So, Tuesday," I manage to say, finishing my drink. I need to leave *right now* because if I don't, I might actually jump into his lap. *I want to give you everything you want.* Yeah ... no guy in his twenties has ever said that to me. Buttons is a full-on zaddy.

"I'll call you with the details."

Call. Not text. The fact that he said "call" hits different.

"Thank you for the drinks," I say, standing up, my head spinning with everything that just happened.

"Can I walk you out?" he offers.

Oh my God ... does he ... are we going to kiss? But how? He's still wearing the mask. He said he wouldn't reveal himself until Tuesday. *Maybe I'll get another clue as to who he really is.* I'm too curious now.

"Sure."

The man in the bunny mask slides off his barstool and immediately takes my hand. I instinctively giggle.

"Too weird?"

"No. What a sight."

He's guiding us toward the back of the bar, not the front. *We are going to kiss!* This is not how I thought today was going to go.

"Is this where you murder me?" I joke.

His chuckle from behind the mask is so deep. He opens the door to the back lot and whispers, "I'm serious about giving you everything you want."

What the fuck is about to happen?!

Outside, the air is cool, and before I can even think, his hand presses me firmly into the wall. My breath catches as I hit the brick exterior.

"Close your eyes."

"No," I tease, testing him, but then his hand covers my eyes, blocking out the world.

"I've had a crush on you for a while."

Smiling, I hope this is Chad.

"What does my little bunny want?"

My lips part in response, and I feel his finger trace them, sending shivers through me.

"You want to kiss a stranger?"

"You're not a stranger."

"You don't know that."

"I have a pretty good idea."

"But you could be wrong," he whispers right into my ear.

"I hope I'm not wrong," I say, my heart racing.

There's some rustling—maybe him adjusting his mask— and I still can't believe I'm standing behind High Five, blinded by a guy in a bunny mask. His other hand wraps

33

around the back of my neck, pulling me forward. And then, I feel his lips on mine.

This is so hot.

His kiss is firm, demanding, and it sends a wave of heat through me. He's completely in control, and I'm loving every second of it. He pulls back, and I'm left breathless.

"I'm looking forward to Tuesday."

"Me too," I breathe, still reeling.

"No peeking. I'm going to go back inside. See you Tuesday."

"I might peek."

"No peeking, baby," he warns.

I chuckle.

"Good context, right?"

"Right," I breathe, still blindfolded by his hand.

"No peeking until you hear the door shut."

"Fine," I agree, biting my lip.

"Say it. Say, 'no peeking until the door shuts.'"

I bite my lip again, very turned on at how much control he's taking. "No peeking until the door shuts."

12

Chad

Re-entering High Five, the bunny mask off and held in my hand, a dumb smile is glued to my face. *Tuesday.* I can't wait to see her again.

"Did you seriously pick up Anna Clark while wearing the bunny mask?" my friend Chris, Lauren's husband, asks, his voice full of disbelief as soon as he spots me.

"Seems that way."

Nicholas laughs from across the table and raises his hand to get Aaron's attention. "We need a pitcher over here!"

"You were a good sport today," Nicholas says, patting my back as I sit at the tall boy table.

Aaron sets down a fresh pitcher of beer.

"I'm taking fantasy football a lot more seriously next year."

Chris leans forward. "Nicholas, you know there's a rumor going around that you're buying an engagement ring."

"What?!" Aaron and I say in near unison.

"That's what I get for supporting local businesses." Nicholas sighs, but there's a glint in his eye.

"You're serious?" I ask, still shocked.

Nicholas smirks and nudges me. "Never underestimate the power of roleplay. It can be life changing."

While I laugh, my mind goes to some very specific places I'd rather not be. *I do not want to think about Emily calling him Santa, and I definitely don't want Anna to call me anything related to the Easter Bunny.*

"When's your next themed pop-up?" I ask, steering the conversation back to safer ground.

"Halloween, for sure," Nicholas says, leaning back. "Still deciding about any other holidays before then. Our social media girl, Taylor—if it were up to her, we would be a permanent pop up." He shakes his head, then takes a sip of his beer. "They're great for extra sales in the off season, but once summer is here, I want this to be High Five. A place where you can grab a cheap beer and hang with your friends."

"Speaking of, we need to do a celebratory shot to close out fantasy season," Chris says.

"I'm not doing a bomb," I firmly state. *Those are in time out for a while.* Hangovers in your thirties are not worth it.

"What do you want then, princess?" Chris teases me.

"I've been through enough torture today. How about a nice whiskey?"

"Whiskey, perfect," Nicholas says. "Claire, three shots of my favorite, please."

"To day drinking," Claire says, returning with the shots. We each pick one up, and she says, "Cheers, boys," raising her own shot glass, and we all tip them back.

"Claire's cute," Chris says, checking her out as she leaves.

"You're married," Nicholas fires back.

"I can still say a girl is cute."

Questionable.

"CB, isn't Claire cute?" Chris asks me.

"Why are you doubling down on this?"

"There is nothing unattractive about Claire, so why can't I say she's cute?"

"What would you think if your wife said Aaron or Chad are cute?" Nicholas tests.

"They are cute ... cute, pretty boys."

I sip my beer as the guys continue their debate. My thoughts drift back to Anna who is *very* cute. I can't stop thinking about her, about how I want to make her feel special, like the only girl in the world.

13

Anna

Sunday, April 20th

M y phone buzzes, and I groan. It's still dark out. *Who's texting me?* I pat my hand on my night-stand, trying not to move my body, until I feel my phone. Grabbing it, I blink one eye open.

UNKNOWN NUMBER
There's something for you outside your door.

It's barely seven thirty in the morning. I'm guessing this text is from my mystery bunny ... Buttons. I hope, at least. I've been getting anxious that I haven't heard from him since we kissed yesterday.

ANNA CLARK
I do not get up this early.

UNKNOWN NUMBER
Nothing is perishable. Get it when you wake up for the day.

ANNA CLARK

I'm too curious now.

Smiling, I roll out of bed and open my door. *An Easter basket!* Picking it up, I take it inside my small, one-bedroom apartment and sit on the couch. Sorting through the items, this is so freaking cute. There's a bunny ears headband, easter candy, fuzzy bunny socks, a bottle of champagne, and a card. Opening the card, there's a print of the photo of me kissing Buttons on the cheek and the same terrible handwriting from the last note.

"Hoppy Easter! Buttons is off duty now.
I'll be picking you up at five on Tuesday."

Smiling, I call the unknown number, and it doesn't even ring twice before it answers.

"Morning," I hear his voice, the same voice of the guy I kissed yesterday. Relieved I don't have a stalker, just a stan, I giggle.

"A little creepy you know my apartment number."

"My friend owns the building."

"Well ... I like that you're a little creepy."

"I think the word you're looking for is cute."

I make a scrunch face, not that he can see it through the phone. But I love this banter.

"It's very sweet. Too sweet. Makes me wonder why you're too single."

He chuckles, and it's silent for a moment.

"I'm looking forward to seeing you on Tuesday ... without the mask," I say.

"I can't wait."

"So ... what are you up to today?"

"Family stuff. Going to have dinner at my parents' house and see my sisters and their families."

He's close with his family too. Nice.

"This really is so cute of you. Thank you."

"Anything for my little bunny."

My cheeks flush, and I love it. I fucking love this strange man flirting with me, buying me gifts, and calling me little bunny. *I really hope it's Chad.*

"See you Tuesday," I manage and hang up. My heart is racing so fast.

"Anna!" my sister greets, opening the door of her house. Cam's squeals and my parents' voices spill out, mixing with the smell of Easter brunch. "Don't you look cute in those bunny ears."

I giggle, excited to tell her about yesterday. "You'll never guess who bought them for me." She cocks a brow as I step inside, homemade lamb-shaped cookies in hand. "The Easter Bunny."

Her eyes widen. "The Easter Bunny?! What?!"

I glance hesitantly into the dining room where our parents are already in full gossip mode. Mom is talking about how nice the church service was with my aunt. We make eye contact, and she brings up how many nice boys there are at church, instantly earning an eye roll. The last thing I need is them getting riled up about another potential suitor. They get too enthusiastic every time I mention a guy, and I can already imagine their reactions. *It's way too soon to tell them about this, especially since I don't exactly know who my potential suitor is.*

"Shh!" I hiss. "Let's not get them involved, okay?"

"He put an Easter basket out front of your apartment this morning?" she asks cautiously.

"Yep. It was really cute."

Megan raises a brow, clearly curious. "How does he know where you live?"

"Oh my God." I swat her arm, laughing. "I did *not* hook up with the Easter Bunny last night! I mentioned it to him at the bar."

She gives me a skeptical look. "You shouldn't tell strangers where you live."

"Everyone at High Five seemed to know him," I say, lowering my voice even more. "I still think it's Chad Braun."

Her eyebrow quirks. "Wait, you still don't know?"

"I'll find out on Tuesday. We're going out."

Her eyes narrow, concern flickering in them as she drops her voice to a whisper. "I'm not loving this, Anna. You're sure it's safe?"

The whispering feels like it's drawing too much attention, so I nod quickly, forcing a reassuring smile. "It's fine. I promise. I just want to make sure before Mom and Dad start planning the wedding."

She snorts. "Fair point. But still, be careful, okay?"

I glance toward the dining room where Mom is already looking our way. *Please don't ask about this*, I silently beg. I'm not ready for a full interrogation.

"Heard," I whisper back, and we both straighten up. I quickly change the subject as we step into the dining room. "The book I'm reading ... I don't think you're going to want to read it once I'm done."

"Why not?"

"The chasing in the woods scene was really intense."

Megan shakes her head. "Why do you like that stuff?"

I shrug, thinking about how fun it would be to reenact some of the scenes I've read.

14

Chad

"Chad, where's my kiss?" Mom asks, moving frantically around the cramped kitchen in my childhood home. This house barely fit the six of us growing up, and now it's almost bursting with ten. I set the bottle of wine on the counter and give her a kiss on the cheek. "One of these days, bring a girl instead of a bottle of wine," she chides, shaking her head as she stirs a pot.

"One of these days, let me make a holiday meal at my house," I quip back. I did offer to host Easter this year, after all. My place is bigger, with an open floor plan, but Mom refused to break tradition.

"When you have a girlfriend." She raises her brow.

Mom's getting impatient with my single life, I know. "If you're lucky, I'll host Thanksgiving."

"If I'm lucky?" She squints at me.

"I'm working on it."

"Good."

"Does that mean you're dating someone?" my oldest sister, Kelly, chimes in, stepping into the kitchen.

"Early days."

43

"You hear that?" Kelly looks at Mom. "He's being vague. That means he likes her. Who is she?"

"You wouldn't know her."

Kelly narrows her eyes a little. "Does she not live around here?"

"She lives here ... in Lake Geneva."

"And I wouldn't know her?"

Do I tell them about how much younger Anna is than me?

As if on cue, Heather, my youngest sister, slips into the kitchen, along with Ashley, who lives for gossip.

"Chad being quiet, now this is intriguing," Heather says.

Being ganged up on by all these women, it's nothing new. I have no choice now. I'll have to tell them every painstaking detail.

"Her name is Anna Clark."

"Megan's sister? Isn't she, like, super young?" Heather immediately responds.

"She's twenty-two."

"Hmm," Heather hums, and I know. Anna is younger than her.

"Anna? Isn't that the girl you've been crushing on for months?" Ashley pokes my stomach. "The reason you're eating so much pasta."

"Yes. That Anna."

"How long have you two been dating?" Mom asks, nearly shrill. "You could have brought her here."

"Mom, we haven't even been out on an official date."

"You've been, what? Netflix and chilling?" Kelly raises a brow.

"No! I finally got the courage to ask her out the other day, so like I said ... early days."

"When are you taking her out, then?" Mom asks, no longer focused on dinner.

"Tuesday."

"Uncle Chad!" My nephew Oliver, Kelly's son, runs in, hugging me. *Thank God!* I toss him onto my shoulders and take that as a cue to leave the kitchen. If I don't leave now, they're going to ask for even more information about Anna.

Beyond stuffed after dinner, I make my way to the couch, dropping down onto the opposite end from Dad. He's got the TV on, his usual post-meal ritual, and will probably be snoring in five minutes. The smell of ham and mashed potatoes still hangs in the air.

"You have to tell us, how was it being the Easter Bunny?" Kelly asks, pacing as she rocks her two-month-old son. "I'm so mad we missed it. These boys are terrible sleepers right now, and I was too drained to go."

"The costume itself was terrible. So hot to wear. But it was a great event."

"I'm sad I missed seeing you as the bunny." My brother-in-law Noah leans on the wall in the living room. "But honestly, if I'd lost fantasy, I'm not sure I could've gone through with it."

"Oh, we would've made sure of it," I say, smirking. "Rules are rules."

"You guys gave me a lot of ideas for my fantasy league," says James, my soon-to-be brother-in-law.

"Next season, are you joining our league or not?" I ask him.

"Depends on what the loser has to do. I think we've been way too nice to each other in our league." He gives Ashley a kiss before sitting on the recliner.

My sisters picked good guys. I know they're right about me needing to take dating more seriously. With how well the bar banter was on Saturday, I'm excited to take Anna out on Tuesday.

"The bunny costume is how I broke the ice with Anna," I admit to the group.

"What do you mean?" Heather perks up, fully invested now as she sits cross-legged on the rug in front of the couch.

"I invited her to High Five to have a drink with 'Buttons the Bunny.'"

"This poor girl," Kelly says, although she's smiling. "Wait—are you saying you wore the costume at the bar?"

"Just the mask."

"And she was into it?" Ashley asks skeptically, taking a seat next to me on the couch.

"Yeah." I shrug. "Apparently."

"Well, you two sound like a match already." Heather laughs.

"I would've been, like, 'take off that mask, weirdo.'" Ashley chuckles, nudging me with her elbow.

"Do you want to hold him?" Kelly asks now that baby Theo is asleep in her arms.

"Give me the little man!" I reach over, taking him carefully. He's tiny, but I'm still cautious with him. "He's big, right? Like longer than most babies this age?"

"He's in the eightieth percentile for height and weight."

"I do not want a ten-pound baby, but it feels inevitable at this point," Ashley says, leaning over and reaching for Theo's hand.

"Inevitable before or after the wedding?" I tease.

"After." She nudges her shoulder into me.

"I'm a little scared of babies when they're this small," I share. "But once they're Oliver's age, it's adventure time with Uncle Chad. Let me know when I can take him off your hands sometime."

"Will do." Kelly smiles at me. "You know, if you took dating more seriously, you could have your own family by now."

I give her a sarcastic look. "Is that how it works?"

But something in her comment sticks with me.

Monday, April 21st

CHAD BRAUN

How is my little bunny doing today?

ANNA CLARK

Good. Just so you know, I still don't have your number saved in my phone because I refuse to add you as Buttons.

CHAD BRAUN

Just one more day of waiting.

ANNA CLARK

I'm working tonight, by the way … do with that information what you will.

She thinks she's so clever. No way I'm going to La Nonna tonight and risk ruining the surprise. But damn, she *is* clever. I usually go there on Monday nights since it's slow. Should I go? *Fuck.*

CHAD BRAUN

Do you want me to show up?

ANNA CLARK

That depends.

CHAD BRAUN

On?

ANNA CLARK

If you flirt with me or not.

Hmmm.

CHAD BRAUN

You want me to show up at your work and distract you?

ANNA CLARK

I think you know it's usually slow on Monday nights.

Clever, clever girl. She's got to know it's me.

CHAD BRAUN

What's the difference between a stan and a stalker? Because I think you're confusing me for the latter.

ANNA CLARK

Well ... you'll know where I'll be later.

I smirk, the possibilities running through my mind. Do I play it cool and tease her? Do I show up at La Nonna and tell her? Or do I skip the whole thing altogether and wait until tomorrow? Decisions, decisions ...

15

Anna

As expected for the off-season, tonight is a slow night. I'm grateful for it, though, because I'm completely distracted, wondering if Chad is going to show up. He doesn't have a set time, but he comes in most Mondays before seven.

It's six now, and I've only had two tables. I still have to work these slow shifts, though—it's the only way to get preferred scheduling in the summer when I can pull in at least five hundred dollars a night. My best night was three grand, but that was thanks to some drunk guys from Chicago trying to impress me and get my number. *Who cares? I'll take the money.* I'm just glad they hired me. Most of the servers here are much older. I'm the youngest.

I take a deep breath as I see Chad walk in. *Okay. Don't make this weird. The bunny might not even be him, and you could be building a whole fantasy in your head. Or ... it is* him. And if that's the case, why is he here? To flirt? To keep up the mystery?

The hostess walks up to me, and I already know what she's going to say. "He requested you."

49

He always does. *Calm the fuck down.*

I approach his table, keeping my voice steady. "Hey, how are you doing?" My standard greeting—nothing weird.

"Hey."

Now that I'm thinking about him as someone I could be going on a date with, I check him out. He always looks good. Never anything embarrassing, and no graphic t-shirts. This henley is nice, cute. His arms look huge and remarkably similar to the bunny's.

Okay, focus. I jump into my usual script for the night, telling him about the specials.

"How about you surprise me?" he says.

Hmm. That's new. He usually orders a variation of the same thing—homemade pasta with one of the house sauces.

"What's your budget?" I ask, trying to keep it light.

"Not worried about that tonight."

"How hungry are you?"

"Starving."

Is this flirty?

"Okay ... but no sending it back to the kitchen if you don't like it."

"I know I'll like it."

This is definitely different energy from him. It has to be him. Stop blushing. It's weird.

I let out an awkward giggle, feeling the heat rise to my face.

"Are you having a Stella, or ...?" I ask, trying to regain some composure.

"Stella."

I quickly walk over to the tablet on the wall and tap in the order. I choose my favorite dish on the menu: lamb shank with potatoes. It's decadent, but amazing. *He'll love it.*

When I set the beer down at his table, I remind myself to keep things neutral. "Did you have a nice weekend?"

"Parts of it were really nice ... other parts were terrible."

"Did you get arrested?" I tease.

"No ... but you could say I was in one form of jail."

I raise my eyebrows, giving him a sassy look. *Just tell me already!* I want to scream.

Chad takes a sip of his beer, and I remind myself I can't spend the whole night at his table. I drift to the back with the other servers. "What do you guys know about Chad Braun? Like, what's the tea?"

"The gossip?" Vicky, one of the older servers, clarifies.

I nod.

"Nice guy. He and his friends used to get up to all kinds of nonsense in their twenties, but he's calmed down a bit."

"What kind of nonsense?"

"Stupid, drunken behavior."

"And what's his reputation with girls?"

She squints at me. "Why are you so curious about him?"

I might be going on a date with him tomorrow.

"He comes in here a lot," I say, trying to sound casual. "I get the feeling he's going to ask me out one of these days."

"I haven't heard much about him," she says, shrugging. "Which is probably a good thing."

I smirk, grabbing his dish from the counter. "Lamb shank with potatoes," I announce, setting it in front of him.

"This looks amazing."

I smile, debating how much more small talk I should make.

"So ... what are you up to tomorrow?" he asks.

If my date tomorrow is with him, he has the greatest poker face of all time.

"I have plans," I say, playing it as cool as I can. "You?"

He glances down before meeting my eyes again. "Too bad."

"Why?"

"I was going to ask you out."

I burst out laughing. Probably not the appropriate response, especially if he's *not* the guy I'm going out with tomorrow.

"Why is that so funny?" he asks, tilting his head.

Am I going to keep playing along? I feel like I might combust from all the tension and confusion swirling around in my head.

16

Chad

I'm so glad I came in tonight. Anna is completely flustered and nervous, and it's the cutest thing ever. She definitely suspects it's me behind the bunny mask, and I love this little teasing game we've got going. I haven't been this excited about a girl in ... years. *Why's that?* Something about her keeps me guessing, keeps me wanting more.

Since she dodged my question and her blushing is too irresistible, I decide to push a little harder. "Are your plans with your girlfriends or another guy?"

"None of your business," she shoots back, her eyes narrowing slightly, but the smile playing on her lips tells me she's still enjoying this.

"So ... a guy," I tease, raising an eyebrow.

She bites her lip, staring intently into my eyes. Damn, she looks good tonight—high ponytail, black long-sleeve t-shirt dress that fits her like a glove. There's a pause, and I can feel the tension hanging in the air between us before she finally answers.

"It's kind of a blind date," she says, her voice almost challenging, as if daring me to react.

I can't stop smiling. The way she teases me back makes her stand out. She's not just playing along—she's actively matching me in this game, and I love it. *Anna is so fun.*

"Who set you up?" I ask, resting my head in my hand.

She covers her face with her hands, giggling, before poking me in the chest. "The Easter Bunny did."

The Easter Bunny did. I laugh and then stay in character, the character of a guy who has no idea what she's talking about. "Random."

"So random."

We share a smile, a moment that feels easy and comfortable.

"Do you want another beer?" she asks, breaking the silence.

"Not tonight," I reply, watching her as she starts to turn away. I don't want her to go yet. "Anna." She pauses, looking back at me. "You look really pretty tonight."

She seems caught off guard. Her usual quick comebacks falter, and there's a softness in her expression. She smiles, a little unsure, and I wonder if she's trying to figure out if I'm serious or still messing with her.

"Seriously."

"You look better than usual for some reason too," she says with a little giggle, then leaves me.

I'm obsessed. Anna Clark's number one stan.

17

Anna

Chad has absolutely no intention of revealing himself. But it's him—I know it. Chuckling to myself, I grab a Sharpie and start sketching a small bunny on the to-go box he's inevitably going to ask for. I add a little thought bubble and write, *See you tomorrow -Little Bunny*.

If I'm wrong, this will be awkward. And if I'm right? Hilarious.

As I approach his table, I force myself to stay calm. "Would you like anything else?"

"For you to go out with me tomorrow."

I blink, caught off guard for a second, but a snappy thought pops into my head. "Why would I bump tomorrow's guy for you?" I tease, though my heart skips a beat. *I know it's him. It has to be him.*

"You sure he's going to give you what you want?"

I sharply inhale, a flash of our kiss replaying in my mind. It was *definitely* with Chad. "I'm confident."

He bites his lip, smirking. "I'll take a to-go box and the check."

To-go box. Perfect. I hold back my own smirk, knowing he's about to see my little surprise.

"You could take me out another night," I tease, keeping the banter alive. And finally—there it is—a crack in his poker face. His smirk falters, and I feel a tiny surge of victory. *Got him.*

The slight twitch of his lips is everything. He recovers quickly, but I see it. I can't help but feel a thrill at finally getting under his skin. He's been playing it too cool this whole time.

As I turn to grab the check, my heart races. *What does he mean by "give me what I want"?* I begin weighing if I should hook up with him tomorrow or not. I think I want to. *Lie.* I know I want to.

I grab the to-go box from the counter, still fighting back a smirk.

Setting the box and the check down in front of him, I wait, watching his face carefully. He picks it up and glances down at it. There's a beat of silence, and then he chuckles, low and deep.

"See you tomorrow, huh?" he asks, staring down at the note.

I shrug, trying to keep my cool, but inside I'm buzzing with anticipation.

He raises an eyebrow, his gaze locking onto mine. "We'll see, won't we?"

As I walk away, I can't stop smiling. *Tomorrow is going to be fun.*

18

Chad

Tuesday, April 22nd

Stepping out of the shower, I towel off my hair, my mind replaying that kiss with Anna. *I really want to kiss her again.* My phone buzzes as I work some product into my hair, taking an extra step tonight to look good.

ANNA CLARK

So, what are we doing? I have no idea
what to wear.

CHAD BRAUN

We might get a little messy, so nothing
fancy.

ANNA CLARK

How messy?

CHAD BRAUN

Well … it depends …

ANNA CLARK

You could try writing full sentences.

Chuckling, I love it. I love her sass, the way she pushes back at me. It makes the banter so much fun.

CHAD BRAUN

Wear jeans and a cute top you wouldn't be upset about if it got stained.

ANNA CLARK

What are you saying? 🫣

I guess that could be read another way.

CHAD BRAUN

Get your mind out of the gutter, little bunny.

I want to surprise her. I don't want to tell her yet that we're going to Main Street Makers Studio for a "sip, snack, and paint" event. She'll love it—once she realizes.

ANNA CLARK

I thought you were taking me out to a nice dinner. Why are you telling me to wear jeans? 🫣

CHAD BRAUN

You will have a nice dinner.

ANNA CLARK

Sus.

Gen Z. So young ... I need to take this slow.

ANNA CLARK

How will I know who you are?

There are so many ways I could answer that.

CHAD BRAUN

I'll be the guy looking overly excited.

ANNA CLARK

What kind of car am I looking for?

CHAD BRAUN

Patience.

I stare at my phone, smiling, but when I don't see any bubbles, I move on with getting ready. She liked the henley last time, so I'll wear my black one tonight with dark wash jeans and boots. Once I'm dressed, I step up into my truck and decide to text her.

CHAD BRAUN

Be on the lookout for a truck. I'll be there in a few minutes.

ANNA CLARK

Didn't expect the Easter Bunny to drive a truck … I was thinking like a lime green Bug.

What to respond ...

CHAD BRAUN

No texting and driving, so I'm driving now.

19

Anna

Even though it's barely fifty degrees out, I'm feeling flirty and put on a little crop top and high-waisted jeans. I want Chad's hands to be all over me. Hopefully, it's Chad. *Please, don't let it be someone else.*

Checking myself out in the full-length mirror in my bedroom, my blonde hair is getting long, almost past my chest, and I've kept it simple with just a little eyeliner and mascara.

Sliding into my oversized denim jacket, my heart races as I stare out the window. Anticipation. I haven't been this excited to go out on a date in forever. All of the butterflies and nervous energy are there. I really want Chad to be the one picking me up and am refusing to entertain the possibility that it could be someone else.

A big, white truck pulls into the lot. *That has to be him.* Grabbing my mini bag and phone, I quickly confirm I have my keys, then head out the door, locking it behind me.

"I *knew* it!" I squeal as I see Chad leaning casually against the passenger door, looking hot in a black long-sleeved shirt, jeans, and boots. Relief and excitement wash over me—thank God it's not some random guy.

"Hey," he greets me, smiling as he extends his arms for a hug. I step into him, immediately noticing how good he smells. Feeling his back, it's strong, and I smile, loving this hug and how little I feel in his arms.

"I'm way less stressed now," I admit, pulling back.

"Why's that?" he asks, still holding onto me.

"You could have been someone else," I say with a small laugh into his chest, but it's the truth.

"Look at me," he breathes, reaching for my chin, lifting it slightly, and *oh my God is that hot.* He stares deeply into my eyes with a little smile on his face before asking, "Looking forward to spending a few hours together?"

"Of course!"

"Me too." He releases my chin and opens the passenger door for me. I step up into the truck and fasten my seatbelt. Relaxing into the seat, I exhale, my heart rate calming.

"Where are you taking me?"

"On a two-minute drive."

I chuckle, loving how he answers my questions in a way that keeps me guessing. As he starts driving, he grabs my hand, playing with my fingers. I stare at his hand, loving it.

"You look really nice," he says, glancing over at me briefly before focusing back on the road.

"You clean up well yourself," I tease, and he shakes his head, maybe amused by me.

We pull into a parking spot on Main Street, and he shuts off the truck. *Where's he taking me?*

"Let's go," he says.

"Where?"

"To our date."

"You're annoying." Although the smile on my face shows how excited and not annoyed I am.

He smirks and gets out of the truck. I take a deep breath before stepping out. On the sidewalk, he grabs my hand again. I like it. Chad is sweet. *When was the last time a guy planned a whole date for me, from pick-up to activity?* I have a feeling this is going to be the best date of my life.

"Oh!" comes out of me as we approach Main Street Makers Studio.

"We're going to paint a little," he says, smiling.

"Fun!" But then I stop walking, a smirk playing on my lips. He furrows his brow slightly, clearly wondering why I've stopped in the middle of the sidewalk. "A very public date you're taking me on," I flirt.

"And?" he asks, looking smug as ever.

"People are going to be talking about you and me being out together," I point out, fully aware of how people in town love to gossip.

"And?" He steps closer, his eyes locking onto mine as his hands find their way to my hips. His voice drops, low and sexy, as he asks, "What's there to talk about?"

I place my hands on his shoulders, leaning into the flirtation. "There could be a lot to talk about."

He exhales loudly, and I can tell I've gotten to him. It makes me smile.

"I'll kiss you later," he whispers, his voice sending a thrill through me as his hands move up a little, touching the exposed skin between my crop top and jeans.

"Why not now?"

"We might not make it to this class."

I nearly squeal because he's right. The attraction between us right now is so intense.

"One little kiss." I pout.

He leans in, but instead of kissing me on the lips, he presses a soft kiss to my forehead. My jaw drops, mock-offended.

"Choose your words better next time."

I swat his chest, giggling. *I love this. I love everything about it.*

Chad takes my hand again and guides us inside.

As I step into Main Street Makers Studio, it's so cool. I've only been in here a couple of times, but the vibe is so Etsy aesthetic perfection. A long communal table sits in the middle, covered with bottles of wine, charcuterie trays, and little easels ready for us to paint. I'm excited to get to know Chad better.

"Chad!" Sarah Anderson, the owner of the studio and the definition of boho coolness, calls across the room, and I blink in surprise as she gives him a hug. *I didn't realize they were friends.* "This is your plus one?" Sarah asks, turning her attention to me. "Hey, Anna!"

"Hey!" I wave back, feeling slightly awkward. There's nothing to be awkward about aside from the fact that Aaron Olson wasn't interested in me and is now dating her. "You and Aaron are so cute together. Maybe I'll see you at La Nonna soon?"

"We should go back! We'll have to do a date night there again."

After Emily and Nicholas get engaged, I have a feeling Aaron and Sarah will get engaged soon after. They're too perfect together.

"I have you and Chad seated right here," she says, pointing to the end of the table near the big windows overlooking Main Street.

Chad leans in. "So public."

Without thinking, I swat his butt in response. It lands harder than I intended, and Chad shoots me a playful look before leaning down to whisper in my ear. "Whatever you do to me ... it's going to happen to you later."

"Like you need an excuse to grab my ass."

He grins, bear-hugging me close. "You're so feisty. I love it."

I giggle, feeling the warmth of his arms around me, loving this easy banter between us.

"Let me make us some snack plates," he says, ending the hug. "Do you want wine?"

"Yes, please," I say, then take my seat in front of the easel.

Chad puts together a plate of cheeses and nuts, placing it in front of me before sitting next to me. I pick up a piece of cheese and hold it to his lips. He bites down, his big brown eyes locked on mine. The bite was intentional, sexy.

"You looked hungry," I say, trying to keep my voice steady, although that bite was hot.

"I am," he replies, not breaking our eye contact. *Oh we're definitely hooking up after this. But still ... where's dinner?*

Just as I'm about to say something, Sarah begins the instructions for our painting. It's a spring-themed piece with bright colors and floral details.

"Mine is going to look like a five-year-old did it," Chad whispers as Sarah talks.

"Mine won't look much better."

We pick up our brushes and start following the steps.

"How do you know Sarah?" I ask.

"She's close with my oldest sister."

"How old are your sisters?"

"Kelly just turned thirty-two, Ashley is almost thirty, and Heather is twenty-seven."

I make a little face, feeling our age gap. "Do any of them have kids?"

"Kelly has two boys. Three and two months."

"Such fun ages."

"Yeah. I love being the fun uncle."

He likes kids. Another point for Chad, I think while painting.

"So concentrated," Chad teases, glancing at me as I furrow my brows in focus.

"I'm trying to do a good job!" I protest, and he chuckles, brushing a streak of paint onto the canvas. As our paintings start to take shape, Sarah finishes her guidance, encouraging us to focus on the details.

"So, Anna ... what should I know about you?"

I hesitate, not sure how deep I should go. "I don't know."

"What do you want to be when you grow up?"

"Am I not grown up?"

"You know what I mean."

"I'm not super career focused. Honestly, I want to meet a nice guy and start a family. Like having my own family is what I want for my life."

I expect some kind of joke or judgment, but instead, Chad squeezes my hand, and there's no judgment. I'm not used to that reaction. Everyone always tells me I should do one of a million other things before I have kids.

"What about you?"

"I don't know if I'm ever going to grow up."

"Peter Pan for life?" I tease.

He shrugs. "I mean, I don't take everything as seriously as most people. I like my job, I like that I get a lot of free time in the off-season, and I don't have grand plans to expand or anything. I'm pretty content."

I look at each one of his brown eyes, not really believing him. Well, not believing the last part. That he's content.

"But are you?"

Chad tilts his head, then his fingers move to his lips. I guess that's a deep question, and I feel nervous and ramble, "I think you're looking for someone to spend your time with."

"I wasn't looking," he says, then pauses. "But you caught my eye."

Corny, I think, but my heart races at his flirtation. "So you've been coming into La Nonna for more than the pasta?"

He just smiles at me, and how did I never notice this dimple on his right cheek before?

"Chad ... you never flirted with me."

"I was getting to know you. And everything I learned, I liked." He squeezes my hand again. "I didn't want it to be weird."

"You're not weird."

"Well ... not creepy weird."

I poke him playfully. "You are a little creepy."

He pokes me back. "We do have a big age difference."

"We do." I nod, hearing my sister's comments before pushing them aside. "But I don't think we need to put pressure on anything. We're two people on a date."

He squeezes my hand again, and I love how natural this all feels. "Do you want to live around here forever?"

"I want to be close to my family. So, unless they all move, I'm here for the long haul."

"Same," he says, nodding. "I like being near everyone. And I really like it here."

We both smile at each other before Chad says, "Your painting looks very close to the example."

"I'm actually surprised it looks decent." Then I smirk. "Can't say the same about yours."

"You are such a brat." His face is really flirty looking though.

I glance at him, the memory of our kiss creeping into my mind. "I can't believe I kissed you ... bunny mask and all. That's so crazy."

"So crazy?"

"Kissing a stranger while blindfolded and pressed against a wall isn't something I do every day."

"You seemed to enjoy it," he says, giving me a flirty look. "I'll do it again sometime."

"Blindfolding me?" I ask, and the look he shoots me. *That could happen.* The tension in the air between us right now ... I can't hold back a smirk. "I like flirting with you," I admit, staring at my painting.

"Me too," he says, his hand sliding onto my thigh. My eyes shift to his hand, imagining it traveling farther, and a thrill runs through me.

I want him.

"When are you going to kiss me again?" I whisper.

"Outside."

Is he telling me to go outside? Or is he saying it will happen when we leave? He stands, and I flash him a nervous look.

"Don't you want to go to dinner?" The chuckle that follows. He's so amused with himself. I shake my head but can't hold back the smirk on my face.

"Anna," Sarah says, getting my attention as I grab for my

painting. "Leave it here. I'll spray them all with a varnish and you can grab them whenever."

I feel Chad's presence behind me and then a hand on my ass.

"Thanks!" I manage, blushing as he squeezes it.

20

Chad

She's such a little flirt. I don't think she realizes how much she's teasing me. I will blindfold her, spank her, and give her everything she wants—but I'm not saying that now, and definitely not here. Squeezing her ass, I remind myself we still have dinner.

Hovering behind Anna, I lean down so my lips are at her ear. "You're killing me," I breathe. "But you need to be a good girl until we get to dinner."

Her nervous giggle is priceless. Holding her hand, we walk out of Main Street Makers Studio. I'm not escalating this right now, even though I want to. She's holding my arm with her other hand, nuzzling into me as we walk. I kiss the top of her head, feeling so happy with how the first part of our date went.

As I reach for the door handle to open it for her, she grabs my hand, pulling it behind her waist. "I want to kiss you," she says, looking up at me.

Say less. I lean down, kissing her, and she releases my hands, wrapping hers around my neck. The connection between us is impossible to ignore, and this kiss is quickly escalating. My hands squeeze her ass as her tongue crosses mine—she has such a great ass. Anna arches into me. I slide my hands under her denim jacket and squeeze her sides, loving the feel of her exposed skin. Pressing her against my truck, we're full-on making out on Main Street, and I don't care. I don't want to stop. She pulls my hair and—fuck, we might need to stop. This could get out of hand quicker than it has. Patience. There's a time and a place.

"We need to eat," I say, barely breaking our kiss.

"No."

I laugh, gently wrapping my hand around her neck and pulling back to meet her eyes. "We need to eat, little bunny."

Her blue eyes give me a sad, puppy-dog look. She wants to keep going, and I do too. But not now.

"Get in the truck," I say, releasing her neck and opening the door for her. As soon as she's in, I jog around to my side, smiling. I climb in and shut the door, then lean over, resting my hand on her thigh. "Are you going to be able to keep your hands off me at dinner?"

She raises an eyebrow, her smirk deepening. "Are you?"

"Probably not." I move in closer, my lips grazing her neck. She shivers under my touch, and I pull back enough to meet her eyes.

"Do you know what I really want right now?" she asks, and I'm ready to give her anything.

"What?"

"A greasy cheeseburger."

I lean back in my seat contemplating what we should do. "I was thinking about taking you somewhere nicer, but eating burgers in the truck and making out sounds like a better idea."

"I agree."

Her smile, her face—I'm obsessed. "Come here." Grabbing the back of her neck, I pull her into me. Kissing her deep, I still can't believe all of this started because of me being Buttons the Bunny. Pulling back, I rub my thumb along her jaw. "So beautiful. Let's go eat. I can't have you starving on my watch."

I start the truck and pull out onto the road, playing with her fingers as we drive. The flirty looks we exchange—I want Anna. More than the sex that's bound to be life changing, I want her to be mine.

She points to a drive-thru, and I pull in. Once we've ordered and grabbed our food, I park the truck in the lot. The smell of fries and burgers fills the cab. I pull a fry from the bag and hold it out to her. "Open."

She parts her lips enough for me to pop the fry into her mouth. "So sexy." I watch her chew, my mind wandering to less innocent places. I lean in for a quick kiss before she hands me a fry in return.

We fall into an easy rhythm, sharing fries, stealing kisses. It's intimate but casual—and so carefree.

"When's your birthday?" I ask between bites of my burger.

"November 7th," she answers, taking a sip of her drink. "Why?"

"Oh." I glance at her, amused but still a little nervous about our age difference. "You're really mature for twenty-two, you know that?"

"I guess."

"Compared to me ... I was living in bars when I was twenty-two."

"I've heard you and your friends used to get up to a bunch of stupid shit."

"We did. Way too much."

She shifts in her seat, facing me. I check her out—she's so beautiful. "Are you a 'waiting until marriage' kind of girl?" I'm more than a little curious.

"No!" She swats my arm.

"I didn't want to assume anything."

"I'm not a virgin if that's what you're asking."

I chuckle, loving how offended she is. "I wouldn't care either way."

"Well ... I'm not."

I smirk and take a bite of my burger, now even more curious about her.

"Have you ever had a serious relationship?"

"Yeah. I think six months counts as serious," she says softly. "We said we loved each other, but I think what I want doesn't align with most twenty-something guys."

"And what do you want?"

"In a perfect world? I'd like to be married and have a baby by twenty-five."

I reach over and squeeze her hand. "I like the idea of having three years of you all to myself," I flirt.

She smiles, then presses a fry to my lips. "You think you're so smooth, huh?"

I could be ready for all of that in three years.

"Anna Clark, I'm falling for your sassy little ass."

"You think it's little?"

"I think it's fucking perfect."

She bites her lip and looks down. "What about you? What's your timeline?"

I shake my head. "I don't have one."

"Right, Peter Pan."

"I mean, I do want kids eventually, but I'm not in a rush." Feeding her another fry, I love this moment. "You know ... most people would probably find this conversation inappropriate for a first date."

"Is this our first date?" she asks skeptically. "I thought the bar was our first date."

"The bar was a date with Buttons, not me."

"Mmm," she challenges. "I think this is our second date."

"Whatever you say, little bunny."

She takes a bite of her burger, chewing thoughtfully. "So, how did you end up owning a boat rental company?"

I lean back, admiring her, ready to tell her anything and wanting to know everything about her too. "I started as a captain in high school—just driving drunks around the lake during the summer. It was good money, so I kept it going. Eventually, I got involved in everything—maintenance, operations, all of it. When the owner wanted to retire, we worked out a deal. Every year, I own more and more, and in five years, I'll own it outright."

"That's pretty cool."

"Yeah, it's been good. He's been a great mentor."

"What's the biggest tip you've ever gotten as a boat captain?"

"A grand."

"What? How?"

"They wanted to fuck on the boat."

"No way." Her jaw drops. "Did you watch?"

"Would you have watched?"

She laughs, but the tone ... "You're a naughty, little bunny." I lean in and she meets me, kissing me sweetly. "I drove the boat ... What's the most you've ever been tipped at La Nonna?"

She bites her lip.

"More than a grand?"

"Three grand."

I whistle. "Damn. Did you go on a date with the guy?"

She swats at me, laughing. "No! I gave him a fake number."

I pull her in for another kiss, feeling the heat between us ramp up again. "You're too cute."

"You're ..."

"Don't be a brat."

"You like when I'm a brat."

I bite my tongue. We're not playing that game. "I like when you're yourself. I like how witty and funny you are."

"I like that you can keep up with me."

I grumble before whispering, "Taunting me is turning me on."

She blushes then chuckles.

"Overall, you do well at La Nonna?" I ask, needing to tone down the flirting. I'm not sleeping with her tonight.

"Better than most of my friends."

"This summer," I start, thinking about how we both have jobs that cater to tourists, "it's going to be tricky."

"Why?"

"We're both going to be busy, but at least we'll be busy on weekends."

"I think you'll find time for me," she flirts.

"I will," I say, pulling her in for a delicate kiss. "That was hard on my ex."

Anna perks up. "Tell me about her."

"Why?" I ask, surprised.

"I'm curious."

"We dated for a couple of years."

"And?"

"She wanted to lock it down, but I wasn't ready."

Anna arches an eyebrow. "And now?"

74

"For the right person, I could be ready." We hold a heated stare. "How do you know you want marriage and kids already?"

"I just do. Plus, I'm like my nephew's second mom, and I love it."

"So, stay-at-home mom?"

"Without the fifties sexism and financial domination."

I laugh. "You've thought about this."

"A lot."

"I don't usually talk about these things, but you've got me curious now. What do you mean by financial domination?"

"If I'm not going to generate income, then your money is our money—the end."

Smirking, I love this. "Are you sure you're twenty-two?"

"Are you sure you're thirty-four?"

"No." I chuckle. "So, did I do a good job with this date?"

"Yes."

"Let me take you home." I start the truck, noticing the look on Anna's face. It's like she's sad. "Baby, what's that face about?"

"You're done with me already?"

I tap my phone to check the time. "Three hours isn't enough for you?"

She nudges her shoulder into mine as I drive toward her apartment. Anna leans over, her hand sliding across my jeans, and I tense. I grip the steering wheel tighter as her hand starts rubbing me over my jeans.

Anna *fucking* Clark.

I narrow my eyes. "Are you teasing me, or are you serious right now?"

She giggles, and I bite my lip. While I'm not complaining, I know tonight's not the night for that. I stop her hand, interlacing her fingers with mine.

"Not tonight."

"Why not?"

"Little bunny, you are not giving me road head right now."

She pouts playfully. "Why not?"

"Trust me, I fucking want it, but ... this is special." We hold a long stare before I look back at the road. "When we go on a road trip, though," I chuckle to myself, "you can."

"Oh yeah? Where are we going?"

Naughty. I never would've guessed she was this naughty. I love it.

"We should go somewhere in the next couple of weeks, before Memorial Day for sure," I suggest, wanting to take Anna on so many more dates. "Where do you want to go?"

She thinks for a second. "I hear southwest Michigan is pretty. I've never been."

"We'll go," I promise. "My schedule is flexible until Memorial Day, so let me know when you can get away for a few days."

"A few days? Like three or four?"

"Yeah."

She smiles, but her face clouds with a bit of hesitation. "I'll have to talk to my sister. I help them out a lot."

"I get that. My youngest sister might be able to help out too."

"Megan's really protective about who watches Cam, but we'll figure it out."

We'll figure it out.

And just like that, I'm making future plans with her. I'd been so on the fence about asking Anna out, I never really considered what would happen if it went well. Tonight is perfect, and I want so much more.

21

Anna

I can't stop smiling. My cheeks actually hurt from smiling so much. This was the best date of my life. When Chad parks his truck in front of my apartment building, my heart races. I don't want this night to be over, but I'm also nervous about what comes next. I want him. Do I ask? Or should I go for it?

I turn toward him, biting my lip, but there's no hesitation when I ask, "Do you want to come in?"

Chad looks conflicted. "I'll walk you to your door." He squeezes my hand before sliding out of the truck.

I blink, a little surprised. Just to my door?

I watch him as he walks around the truck, my mind racing. Why doesn't he want to come in? We've been flirting and kissing all night—the chemistry between us is undeniable. Right? When he opens the door for me, I hold eye contact with him as I step out.

"Don't look so sad."

"I'm not sad." But I know I don't sound convincing. "Come inside." The words slip out again, a bit more insistent this time.

Chad smiles but shakes his head. "No."

"Chad," I press, feeling the heat rise in my cheeks. He grabs my hand, and we silently walk to my unit.

"That sad face is killing me," he says as we near my door.

"Why don't you want me?" I ask, looking down.

Before I know what's happening, his hand is around my neck, and I'm slammed into my front door. "Are you serious?" he breathes, looking down at me—and fuck, am I wet right now. That was hot. "I want you, Anna."

"So come inside," I pant, his big hand covering my throat, applying the slightest pressure. Staring up at him, feeling so small beneath his height and presence, I'm weak. He has to be able to feel my pulse and how fast my heart is beating.

"Not tonight, little bunny."

"Why not?" My voice comes out more breathless than I want, frustration bubbling beneath the surface. His thumb brushes gently along the side of my neck. No one has ever done that to me before.

"Because you're special."

I huff, louder than I mean to, crossing my arms as I feel my body practically shaking with need. Why do I have to be special? Why can't he want to fuck me without thinking about what happens next? I want him so bad, and his hand around my neck is not helping me calm down.

"You're trying to wife me up," he grumbles. "What kind of girl would I be if we slept together right now?"

I giggle despite the frustration simmering inside me, uncrossing my arms. He squeezes my neck a little, pressing me back against the door more, getting closer to me, and my pulse skyrockets.

"I think," I say, barely getting the words out because I

am so fucking turned on, "you'd be the kind of girl who has her cake and eats it too."

His lips crash into mine, his hand still firmly wrapped around my neck. It's the kind of kiss that makes me think he's changing his mind. The kind of kiss that says more is going to happen. This kiss has me breathless and wanting to pull him back in when he breaks away.

"I hate you," I breathe, though my body is arching into him.

His fingers stroke my neck, turning me on more as we stare at each other.

"You're mean," I pant as he releases my neck.

"I want you ... I really fucking want you. Trust me." He brushes a stray lock of hair from my face. "Let me be a gentleman tonight ... so I can not be one the next time I see you."

My heart practically leaps out of my chest, and somehow, I manage, "Okay."

"When's your next free night?" he asks, interlacing our hands.

"Thursday," I breathe, my mind already fast-forwarding. Two days ... too many days. Why do I have to wait two more days?!

"Thursday. I'll make dinner."

I raise an eyebrow, trying to play it cool even though I'm sweating, wet, and considering mauling him. "Where do you live?"

"I'm picking you up. Then, you'll see."

"So, you want me trapped at your house?"

He leans in closer, his lips grazing my ear as he whispers, "You're dropping a lot of hints that you want me to kidnap you."

I laugh. "No, I'm just being funny."

"Sure," he murmurs, pressing his lips to my neck in a slow, deliberate kiss. "Thursday. I'll grab you at six."

I raise an eyebrow. "Grab?"

"There will be lots of grabbing." His eyes darken with a promise.

I hold his gaze, unable to stop myself from smiling. "What else?"

"Whatever you want."

"I'm holding you to that."

"Please do."

I smirk, my mind already racing ahead to Thursday, imagining what could happen, what I want to happen.

"See you on Thursday." He leans in for one last kiss, this one slow, tender, and sweet. Both of his hands cup my face, making me feel all the good butterflies. As he pulls away, he commands in a low voice, "Go inside."

22

Chad

I need a fucking shower. My heart's still racing as I sit in my truck, blankly staring out. My willpower has never been more tested. That was the right decision. Was it? It was!

Exhaling loudly, I start the truck and begin driving home. Little, fucking bunny is marriage material. I can't even believe I'm thinking that—thinking about all of that. But I want it. I don't think anyone is ever going to make me feel the way Anna does. I don't think I'm ever going to want anyone more than I want her. I'm down bad for this cute, naughty, needy, sassy, fucking girl.

Thursday. I've never looked forward to anything more in my life.

23

Anna

Wednesday, April 23rd

Confirming I have my keys, I open the door, ready to spend the day babysitting Cam. But then I stop short, gasping. "Oh my God," I squeal, seeing a gorgeous bouquet of lilies sitting right on my doorstep. "Chad."

I pick up the bouquet, inhaling the fresh scent as I bring it inside and set it on the kitchen counter. Staring at the flowers, the biggest smile grows on my face. *He's the best.* I've never been showered with gifts like this, never felt this special. Opening my text thread with him, I start typing.

ANNA CLARK

Oh no.

CHAD BRAUN

What?

ANNA CLARK

You have competition.

I chuckle at my own message, glancing back at the lilies.

The truth is there's no competition. Chad's been on my mind constantly, and with tomorrow's date approaching, the anticipation is practically killing me.

CHAD BRAUN

Read the card.

I notice the card tucked into the bouquet and pull it out. As I open it, I laugh to myself.

ANNA CLARK

It's hard to read. Your handwriting is bad.

"I can't wait to see you tomorrow. Don't dress up. Wear yoga pants or something comfy."

I smirk, biting my lip.

ANNA CLARK

So you just want to stare at my ass. Got it.

CHAD BRAUN

More than stare.

Oh my God. The way he flirts, the way he knows exactly how to get under my skin—now I'm turned on.

ANNA CLARK

We talked about this. Your sentences …

CHAD BRAUN

You're sassy this morning. I think you need a spanking. (Two full sentences 😏)

Run, Little Bunny

Spanking?! My heart races, the heat rising in my cheeks. Too nervous to continue the flirting, I ask another question.

ANNA CLARK

What are you up to?

CHAD BRAUN

I'm at the gym.

That's a hot mental image.

ANNA CLARK

Send a sweaty selfie when you're done.

He sends a thumbs-up reaction, and I place my phone down, glancing back at the flowers. *He really knows how to make me smile.* But before I can get too lost in the thought, I remember I need to head to my sister's house to watch Cam.

Sliding into my little car, I take a few deep breaths to calm myself. *Chad has me all worked up.* My mind keeps drifting back to tomorrow. What does he have planned? What's he going to spoil me with next?

Pulling into my sister's driveway, I flick the key, turning off my car. As I'm about to head inside, my phone buzzes. I nearly drop it when I see Chad's sweaty mirror selfie. He's in a tank top, flexing his bicep. Whoa. Hot. And those shorts. I giggle to myself. *At least he doesn't skip leg day.*

ANNA CLARK

Zaddy.

CHAD BRAUN

You'll be panting a variation of that word tomorrow.

I instantly blush, and a giddy laugh escapes me. *Oh my God, this man.*

As I walk toward my sister's front door, still typing, I send him another message.

ANNA CLARK

I was expecting shirtless.

CHAD BRAUN

Tomorrow.

That single word is on repeat. *Tomorrow.* The anticipation is making me feel like I'm about to burst. *Tomorrow can't come fast enough.*

I hear Cam's voice pulling me out of my thoughts. "Anna!"

Looking up from my phone, I see him and my sister standing there. Megan is giving me that look, the one that says, *I'm annoyed but not surprised.*

"You're late," she says, her voice sharp as she walks straight out the door and toward her car.

I'm only a couple of minutes late. I scrunch up my nose and stick out my tongue, making a mock face like we're kids again. Megan's eye roll says *you're still not cute,* but I can't help but smile.

"Oh," she says, gripping the car door handle, a smirk slowly spreading across her face. "Mom called me this morning, asking if I knew who you were making out with last night on Main Street."

Shit. My stomach drops.

"I told her I didn't know who it was," she adds, her smirk now full-blown, a mischievous giggle escaping her as she slips into her car.

Good thing Chad was a gentleman last night, so I won't have to lie by omission when I tell my mom about the date. She'll call—probably any minute now.

"What should we do this morning?" I ask Cam, stepping into their home, trying to shake off the nerves that Megan so expertly set off.

"I want to watch TV," he says, already plopping down on the couch.

"For a few minutes," I say, turning it on and snuggling next to him, trying to focus on the cartoon. But my mind is already wandering again. *Chad.*

I glance at my phone, and an impulsive idea strikes. "I have to go potty. Be right back," I tell Cam as I dart to the bathroom. I lock the door and pull up the picture Chad sent —sweaty, hot.

Biting my lip, I pull my shirt up to my bra and snap a quick picture. My heart races as I hit send.

His response is almost immediate.

CHAD BRAUN
Don't be such a tease.

ANNA CLARK
You started it!

I can't stop smiling. It's like everything is leading to tomorrow. The connection we have—the banter, the flirting —it's all so effortless, so fun. I can't remember the last time I felt this giddy, like I'm back in high school, sneaking texts during class.

"Anna! You didn't flush!" Cam shouts from the living room, jolting me back to reality.

Oops. I quickly flush, even though I didn't actually go, and head back out to the couch. "Snack?" I ask as I pass by.

"Apple slices," Cam says, his eyes glued to the TV.

I grab the apples from the fridge, but as I slice them, my mind drifts back to Chad. I'm so turned on right now, it's ridiculous. I grab a slice and, on a whim, snap another picture—this time of me sucking on the apple.

ANNA CLARK
I'm babysitting, so all I can be is a tease.

CHAD BRAUN
I like these photos.

I know exactly where this is going.

ANNA CLARK
How much?

CHAD BRAUN
I'm thinking about all the ways I can spoil you.

Spoil me? My excitement surges as I imagine what he has planned. What does "spoil" mean to Chad? Is it more flowers? Something sexier? My heart races thinking about it.

ANNA CLARK
So, I should anticipate another early morning present?

CHAD BRAUN
Yes.

A smile is glued to my face. I love being spoiled. I love how Chad is already spoiling me in ways I hadn't even expected.

ANNA CLARK
When do you wake up?

CHAD BRAUN
Six.

Run, Little Bunny

ANNA CLARK

Gross.

CHAD BRAUN

I thought the same thing at twenty-two.

I laugh out loud, sinking back into the couch beside Cam, trying to focus on the TV, but I'm lost in my thoughts about Chad. Like clockwork, my phone vibrates—my mom. *Here we go.*

"Morning," I answer, wandering into the kitchen to not disturb Cam's show.

"Anna. Really?" she immediately scolds, and I'm grateful for Megan's heads up.

"What?" I ask, feigning innocence.

"Who's this guy you're kissing on the street? Is this what you were whispering about with Megan on Easter?"

I smirk, thinking about our kiss. "The guy is Chad Braun. We've been on a couple of dates. He's really sweet and funny."

"Braun," she repeats slowly. "The guy that owns the boat rental company? He's older than Megan." Her tone is full of that familiar, not-so-subtle judgment.

"Yes, and I know." I brace myself for more.

"How did you meet him?"

"He's one of my regulars at La Nonna."

"Hmm," she hums, clearly unimpressed. I can practically see her wrinkling her nose in disapproval.

"He sent me flowers this morning," I add, hoping to steer the conversation in a more positive direction.

"Oh?" Her tone softens. *Of course, flowers make everything better in her book.*

"He's very sweet."

"We like nice boys."

I hold back a laugh, thinking about the times Chad's hand has already squeezed my neck. *Nice boy* might not be the first term that comes to mind. Still, I nod along with her. "He's a nice boy."

Thank God he didn't come in last night.

"So, when is this nice boy taking you out again?"

"Tomorrow."

"Are you excited?"

"Very. But don't start planning the wedding yet," I tease.

24

Anna

Thursday, April 24th

The moment I wake up, I practically jump out of bed hoping there is a surprise outside my door. Opening it, I see my painting from our date along with a little gift box. *Little boxes.* That typically means something really nice. A delicate, gold, chain bracelet with a little, gold bunny charm is inside. *Is this real gold?* Holy shit!

Whether it is or not, it doesn't matter. This is the sweetest gift I've ever received. I clasp the bracelet on my wrist, admiring how it looks. *It's perfect.* Chad is a nice boy I think, chuckling to myself.

I immediately call my sister. *I have to tell her.*

"Morning," she answers.

"So ... I know you have a few thoughts about Chad, but he's the sweetest guy ever."

"Why do you say that?"

"He's been leaving little presents for me, and this morning, I found the cutest bracelet at my door."

"Bracelet?! Who knew he was such a romantic? That's cute."

"Yeah, it's got a little bunny charm, which is his nickname for me."

"Anna and the Easter Bunny." She laughs. "Aren't you happy I pushed you?"

"Pushed me?"

"To take a photo with him ... to go to High Five."

"Thank you." I roll my eyes, even though she's right. I needed the push. Megan sighs. "What?"

"This is really great ... I'm just missing my guy."

"Only two more months to go," I encourage.

"It can't go by fast enough, but I'm excited for you and happy you also sound very eager about all of this."

"I am. Chad's making me really happy."

"As long as he keeps making you this happy, then I don't have any issues with him. But the second he does something ..." Megan giggles.

"You will key his truck. I know."

I squeal, staring at the bracelet, loving it so much.

"When are you seeing him again?" she asks.

"Tonight."

"Have fun."

I'm going to have too much fun. But I am not telling Megan that. "I will. Bye."

I decide to call Chad instead of texting him. This gift is so sweet, and I want him to hear how much I like it.

"You're up early," he answers.

"Your little bunny loves this bracelet."

"I'm happy you like it."

"When did you get it?"

"Yesterday ... I was thinking about you all day."

"Same." I think about his gym selfie. "That photo was very distracting."

"So were yours."

It's silent, and I feel flushed

"I have a photo request," he says.

Oh my God. "It's a little early for nudes, Chad."

"Says who? But I want something nice."

"Like?"

"A selfie of you wearing the bunny ears I got you. I want to make it your contact photo."

"That's going to be embarrassing when other people see it."

"Nah. It's going to be the cutest thing ever."

"Only because I like this bracelet so much."

"I'm happy you like it."

"When are you *grabbing* me?"

"How about six?"

"There better be lots of grabbing."

"My hands will be on you the whole night."

"Good. See you at six."

25

Chad

When Anna exits her apartment with a big bag slung over her shoulder, I do a double take. I know we've been saying this is going to happen. But seeing this bag ... it does something to me. I wasn't assuming that, but damn, I'm happy.

"Give me that bag, little bunny," I say, hopping out of the truck and extending my hand. She passes it over, and I pull her in for a kiss. "I've been wanting to do that all day," I say when our lips part. "You look so cute in this hoodie and yoga pants. I've never seen you so casual."

"I'm good at following instructions." She smirks, staring up at me. "And I guess you look alright."

I look down at my jeans and t-shirt. "Just alright?"

"The hat is my favorite part of your look."

"Do you like the Packers?"

"Sort of ... but I like guys in hats." Her eyes rake down me, and a smirk grows on her face. "The tank top and shorts are a better look on you though." She winks.

So sassy.

"Get in this truck so I can start grabbing you."

As she steps up, I swat her ass. She giggles in response, and now I'm smiling like an idiot. Anna is so perfect for me. Holding her hand as we drive out of town, I'm trying to keep it together, making small talk, hearing about her day, but my mind's racing ahead, imagining how the night's gonna go. I want everything to be perfect.

"And this is where you murder me," Anna jokes as we turn into my long, gravel driveway.

I laugh, glancing at her. She's smiling, but her eyes are scanning the trees on either side of us. "Do you read a lot of true crime or something?"

"Dark romance."

"Dark romance? What's that?" Every time I think I've got her figured out, she surprises me.

"Big dick sexy criminals with stalker tendencies that know how to fuck."

The things that come out of her mouth. She's trying to keep a straight face, but her little smirk is growing and she's too fucking cute.

"And this is popular?"

"Very."

I shake my head, smiling. "I guess I'll have to kidnap you for real, then."

The look on her face. She loves that idea. "So naughty, little bunny. But it's happening now. Sleep with one eye open."

"Don't kidnap me." She swats my arm.

"You want it. Admit it."

Anna bites her tongue. *She's incredible.* While I'd love to rip her pants down and have my way with her against the door when we walk inside, I also want more than that. Talking with her feels so damn good.

Pulling into my garage, I cut the engine and look over at

Anna's blue eyes. They're so beautiful. "Ready to have me wait on you for a change?"

She giggles, and I grab her bag.

"After you." I gesture for her inside.

"This is cute!" she says, looking around.

"You're surprised?"

"I was expecting dead animals on the walls and mismatched furniture ... but this is like a real home."

"Pretty good for Peter Pan?"

"Astounding for Peter Pan," she teases.

I love that she's impressed.

"This is mid-century?"

"Yeah. Built in the '70s, with the right amount of character."

"I like that it's, like, a cabin in the woods."

"Because you want to be kidnapped and taken to a cabin in the woods?"

She laughs softly. "This would be a really nice place to be tied up."

"Anna," I growl. "Be careful about what you say."

"Why? Because you're going to give me everything I want?"

She's such a brat, and I love it. Does she really want all that? Fuck. I might have to propose. Are we really that aligned? "Taunting is a dangerous game," I whisper.

"You said your hands would be on me all night. Are you a liar?"

"Full brat tonight?"

"You bring it out of me."

A low grumble of exasperation and desire leaves me. "I want to be romantic, and you're begging me to bend you over and punish you."

Her face flushes a deep red, and I kiss her again. "Nothing to say now?"

"I think ... we should focus on dinner," she stammers, her face still hot.

"Good plan," I agree, leaning down to kiss her again. I point to the leather couch in the living room. "Go relax. I'll put your bag in my room. Do you want wine or something?"

"What are you making me for dinner?"

"I thought I'd feed you pasta for a change." I wink and head toward the hallway.

"Then, red wine," she says, settling onto the couch, her eyes following me.

"Be right back."

I didn't want to make anything too complicated, especially since ... well, distractions are definitely on my mind. And she's already distracting.

"Are you a clean freak?" she calls from the living room.

"No."

"This place is serial killer clean."

I chuckle to myself. *Why does she keep circling back to that?* "I had my cleaning lady come by this morning to make sure it wasn't a gross bachelor pad."

"I doubt it's ever gross if you have a cleaning lady."

Debatable.

Tossing her bag onto the bed, I loudly exhale. I'm excited but nervous about sleeping with her, not because I don't want this, but because I do—*so* much. This isn't a hookup. Tonight is so much more than that.

26

Anna

C had hands me a glass of wine and leans down, placing a baby kiss on my lips. "Time to make you dinner," he says, pulling back and heading toward the kitchen.

Even though I can see the kitchen from the couch, I stand and follow him. I want to be closer.

"You're going to be my sous chef?" he teases.

"No. I'm going to watch from the front row."

He smirks, opening cupboards and gathering what he needs. I hop up onto the countertop, my legs swinging with nervous energy. I take a sip of wine, trying to calm down, but I love this.

Watching him move around his kitchen, I start to fantasize about a future with Chad—us cooking meals together in this gorgeous, homey space. I didn't expect his home to be this nice, but I feel so comfortable here.

Chad steals a sip of my wine as he passes by, then leans in and kisses my forehead. Am I dreaming? He's being too damn cute. I replay our flirty moment from earlier. This man is not vanilla. Chad is going to fuck me like I've never been fucked—and I'm not mad about it. Smirking, I take another sip of wine.

"Where's your drink?" I ask, surprised he hasn't poured himself a glass or grabbed a beer.

"I can't handle another distraction right now."

I smirk, and we fall into a comfortable silence. As he stirs the meat sauce, I ask, "How long have you had this place?"

"Almost a year," he says, focused on the sauce.

"What made you decide to get a place out here, so tucked away?"

"I wanted something quieter," he says, focused on the sauce. "Renting was fine, but after bouncing from place to place, I realized I wanted something more permanent. Something that was mine."

"I get that," I say, then decide to share, "I've been in my apartment for two years."

Chad turns, catching my eye. "So, you're good at commitment?"

"When I really like something, I am." I smirk, playing into the double meaning.

He chuckles, but there's a new heat in his eyes. The space between us feels charged again, and I can't help but add, "Also ... where are your hands?"

His eyes darken as he steps toward me. "I'm sorry I don't have more hands." He moves closer, his hand sliding up to the back of my neck, pulling me in for a kiss. His lips are soft but firm, and when his fingers curl into my hair, I moan.

"I like that you're needy," he breathes, his lips hovering above mine.

I inhale sharply, my heart racing. His touch, the way he's looking at me—it's too much and not enough at the same time. "You're turning me on so much. How else am I supposed to act?"

Chad smiles, but the intensity in his eyes stays. His hands slide down to my thighs, his fingers press into my yoga pants as he spreads my legs. Every inch of me is on fire. I raise my glass to my lips, trying to calm the shaking inside me. I take a slow sip, savoring this, holding his gaze over the rim of my glass.

"I want you to be comfortable," he says, his voice low.

"I am." Though I've never felt this kind of tension before. It's so hot. I'm literally sweating through my shirt.

He inches closer, his fingers tracing a slow line along the inside of my thigh. "Good. I don't want you to hold anything back. I want to know where your mind is at."

Biting my lip, I decide to be honest. "Right now, I'm thinking about whether or not you're going to fuck me on this countertop."

Chad's hands tighten on my thighs. "Thinking about it more now." He grazes his fingers higher up my legs. The teasing—gosh, I'm so fucking wet. "But I want to do a few other things before we get to that."

"What things?" I manage to ask, my heart pounding.

He leans in, his lips brushing against my neck. "Feeding you," he whispers.

"And?" My voice is shaky.

His lips trail lightly over my neck. "Making you scream."

I exhale, flushed and breathless. "I approve," I whisper back.

He crashes his lips into mine, the kiss deep and hungry. His hands grip my thighs tighter, and I'm sure we're about to go there—right here, right now. But then he pulls back, his hand sliding up to cup my chin. He squeezes it lightly, forcing me to meet his eyes.

"Back to part one," he says, teasing, his lips inches from mine. "I need to plate the food."

I let out a frustrated laugh, but I can't stop the smile spreading across my face. "You're mean."

"I'll make it worth the wait." Chad presses one last lingering kiss to my lips before pulling away.

I watch him as he moves back to the stove, my heart still racing. Pulling off my hoodie, I know the real fun is just getting started.

27

Chad

This is exactly why I couldn't have made anything that required serious attention—dinner would be burnt by now. I glance over my shoulder at Anna as I finish plating. Obsessed is an understatement.

"Take your pretty, little self over to the dining table." With two plates in hand, I watch her slide off the counter. My eyes flick down, staring at the way her hips sway as she walks ahead of me. *That ass.* I'm going to need to spend a lot more time worshiping that.

"More wine?" I ask.

"Only if you're having some."

I smirk and grab a glass, bringing the bottle to the table, refilling hers, and pouring myself one. "Cheers, little bunny."

"Cheers, Buttons."

"Don't remind me."

She giggles. "I was really happy when I saw that the Easter Bunny was buff."

"You think I'm buff?"

"Don't be so desperate for a compliment."

"I was being serious."

"Um. Yeah. Have you seen your arms?"

Smiling, I spin a forkful of pasta, lifting it to my mouth. "I think they could be bigger."

Anna sips her wine with a little chuckle, and I smirk. I grab for her wrist. "I really like this bracelet. When I saw it, I couldn't believe how perfect it was for you."

"It's the best gift ever."

Watching her, I can't believe this. How comfortable tonight feels. Anna twirls her pasta on her fork, using a spoon to assist, and I smile.

"Did they give you pasta eating lessons at La Nonna? You're making me feel like uncultured swine."

"I've learned a lot working there. Especially about wine. Can you believe people actually buy wine that is over a thousand dollars a bottle?"

"No. I mean, I believe it, but I don't get it."

"Same. Like if I was going to blow a thousand dollars, it wouldn't be on a bottle of wine."

"What would it be on?"

"Hmm ... how frivolous am I being?"

"The most frivolous."

"I've always wanted ..." she trails off.

"What?"

"I'm not going to tell you. I don't want you to think that I think you're going to buy it for me."

"Understood. But I don't have that much money, so don't get your hopes up."

She laughs. "Okay. If I was going to light a thousand dollars on fire, I would get these really sexy shoes I keep seeing online. What about you?"

"Hard to say. I guess VIP tickets to Country Thunder."

"You would still go to that?"

"Why wouldn't I?"

"It seems like something high school kids and people in their early twenties do. All of my friends go every year, getting blackout drunk while walking through the mud and singing country music."

"I don't get blackout drunk anymore, but all of that sounds fun to me."

"I've only blacked out a couple of times. I like to have a couple of drinks and then call it."

"Good to hear someone is responsible in this relationship."

"You're not responsible?"

"More than I've ever been, but my gut instinct is to not be responsible."

"Well, I'm not going to put up with much bullshit."

"You shouldn't." I smirk, squeezing her hand.

After a few more bites, she pushes her chair back and stands. Anna moves next to me, her fingers running up my arm as she leans in for a kiss. I push my chair back, and before I know it, she's straddling me.

"After we sleep together," she says, her arms wrapped behind my neck, playing with my hair, "are the gifts going to stop?"

I run my hands down her back, resting them on her hips, taking her in. "So, you're dating me for the gifts?"

"No, but they are so cute. I love them."

"They'll keep coming. More for special occasions versus at your door every day. I can't have you get too spoiled."

She leans in, and I kiss her deep, fisting her hair when her tongue grazes mine. The pant that comes out of Anna is too hot. Moving my hands to her ass, I squeeze and pick her up, walking with her in my arms as we kiss. I don't want to slow down anymore. I lay her on the couch, and she smiles. My heart melts.

"What do you want?" I tease, hovering above her.

"Your hands and lips all over me."

We work together to pull off her shirt and bra. "So perfect," I breathe before my lips explore her chest and stomach while my hands run along her arms. My lips move to her neck, and I like the floral perfume she's wearing tonight.

"Tell me about your fantasies," I whisper.

Anna nervously giggles, shifting a little under me. I smile against her neck as I kiss. God, she's so fucking cute.

"They must be interesting if you're nervous to tell me." I plant a soft kiss right below her ear.

"I haven't done that much," she whispers. "Everything's been pretty vanilla."

I pull back slightly, meeting her gaze. "And you'd like to do more?"

She nods, her lips parted. Seeing her like this—so vulnerable—that makes my heart race.

"Tell me, little bunny." I smirk at the nickname. "But know that whatever you say ... I'm going to make it happen."

"Yeah right." She laughs, but there's a challenge in her eyes.

What are her fantasies? Now I'm really curious. I don't break eye contact as I gently kiss her. "I live to satisfy."

She raises an eyebrow. "Then why are you single?"

I let out a low chuckle, kissing her collarbone as I trail my fingers up her thigh. "Not everyone's worth it."

Her body tenses, and I pull her closer, my lips against her ear. "But you're worth it, Anna." I can see her holding back a smile. "Don't hold back. Give in to everything."

She shrugs. "I'm not used to this kind of intensity."

I pause, looking down at her perfect body sprawled out beneath me. I sweep a strand of hair away from her face. "I'm going to spoil the shit out of you. Maybe even ruin you." I run my hand slowly down her waist, letting my fingers trail over her hips. "This perfect body ..."

She lets out a small noise, like she's disagreeing with me, and I stop.

"You don't believe it?" I ask, sitting back slightly. She shrugs, avoiding my gaze, and that does something to me. I don't like that she doesn't see what I see.

"I've gained a few pounds working at La Nonna."

"And?"

"I want to lose them."

"Where am I going to grab and bite? You have to think about me here too."

"I have to think about you?" The edge in her voice is unmistakable.

"Anna." My voice is soft but firm. "You have a perfect body. The way your waist curves, your ass, these thighs ..." I grab her leg gently, my fingers pressing into her skin. "These thighs I could sink my hands into." I move my hand up to her chest, brushing it lightly. "These perky fucking tits. You have the sexiest body and the most beautiful face."

"This is the biggest I've ever been," she says softly.

"What if I like you exactly how you are? Because I do."

"What if I don't like it?"

"I guess I'll have to live with a smaller ass."

"It will be just as sassy. Don't worry."

Grumbling, I flip her over and swat her ass.

"I'm so turned on right now," she breathes out before giggling.

"What's so funny?"

"How much I like all of this ..." Anna trails off, nestling back into the couch so she's on her back.

I kiss her and then explore her body with my lips. "Touch yourself," I whisper. "Tell me about your fantasies."

Her breath hitches, and she bites her lip again. I can see her hesitating, but I want her to let go.

"Be a good girl," I murmur, my lips brushing her ear again. "Touch yourself."

She covers her eyes with her hand, and I lean back, watching her.

"What?" I ask, needing to know what's going through her mind.

She peeks at me through her fingers, giggling softly. "I've only ever read about guys saying 'good girl.' You're the first guy to say it to me. I like it ... way too much."

Fuck. I bite my lip, trying to keep my composure. "You like it way too much?" I breathe against her neck before kissing and sucking. "That's ... that's turning me on."

She exhales softly. "You want me to touch myself?"

"Yes." I press my body against hers, my lips trailing along her skin. "I want to hear your noises. I want to watch you."

"What are you going to be doing?"

"Kissing every inch of you," I whisper, letting my hand drift down her body.

"Every inch?" she asks, a teasing smile playing at her lips.

"Almost every inch." My voice drops lower. "I want you to be so turned on, little bunny. And I really want to know your fantasies."

She hums, like she's considering it, but there's still a bit of hesitance.

"How about I try to guess them?" My fingers trace lazy circles on her thigh.

She meets my gaze, her lips curling into a smile. "Okay."

We stare at each other for a moment, the tension thick between us.

"Where's my good girl?"

Her smirk deepens as her hand starts to slide down her body. *There she is.*

"I hate how much I like this," she whispers.

"Then you're really going to hate how much I'm going to make you scream. Giving you everything you've ever wanted."

She rolls her eyes at me, her sass making me want her even more. I kiss her harder, my tongue teasing her lips. Her eyes flutter shut, and she makes slow circles on her clit.

"I think you fantasize about ..." I pause, thinking. I have a good idea, but I want my first guess to be funny. "... me putting on the Easter Bunny costume and railing the shit out of you?"

She bursts out laughing, her whole body shaking against mine. "Absolutely not!"

I laugh too, kissing her stomach. I lick and kiss my way up her body, taking in the way her body reacts to every touch. "I think you fantasize about being chased in the woods."

Her eyes flicker open, and she lets out a small hum.

Damn. I knew she had a little inner freak. "I think you want me to sneak in ... start having my way with you while you sleep. You waking up to it."

She bites her lip, her eyes already telling me before she says, "I like that idea."

I smirk, pressing my lips to her ear. "What about it do you like?"

"The fear, then the thrill."

"Added to our to-do list."

She giggles, and I love the sound of it. "I lock my door every night," she says, a little strained, and I'm happy she's turned on, getting closer to coming.

"I like a challenge."

"Now I'm going to have to look cute before bed each night."

"You're always cute. Maybe you should think about ways to make it harder for me to make it happen."

"You're serious."

"Yes, little bunny." I lean in, my lips against her ear. "One of these days, you're going to wake up with my cock inside you."

She moans softly, and I admire her—she's driving me insane with just her reactions.

"We're going to have so much fun together."

She's already squirming under me, and I'm not about to stop kissing and caressing her.

"I think you fantasize about sneaking away ... having a secret quickie, and then returning to the party like nothing happened." Her breathing quickens. "Close your eyes. Focus on this moment right now."

I pull down her yoga pants and start licking and kissing her inner thighs. "Come for me, baby."

She pants in response, and I'm in love. I love how playful and fun she is. I love how sexy she is. I love every second we've spent together.

"You are so special," I breathe, kissing up her body. "Keep making those noises."

"Touch me," she pants, and I smile, moving my hand down her body.

Squeezing her inner thigh, I take all of her in. "Do you need something inside?"

"Yes!"

Sliding a finger in, yeah—I'm in love. She's fucking drenched. I add another finger, slowly going in and out, staring at her face, her flushed cheeks and her closed eyes. Anna's so fucking beautiful. "I'm obsessed with you. I don't want you to leave."

She giggles, ragged. "Maybe I won't."

"If you sleep over, you are not going to get much sleep."

"If?" She exhales loudly. "I'm so close."

I pick up the pace, fucking her faster with my fingers. When she cries out in the sexiest noise I've ever heard, I love it. I love that noise. I love feeling her pulse on my fingers. I start kissing her lower stomach, delicately and deliberately, ready to taste her once she recovers. I want her to come again. I want her to come so many times tonight that she loses count.

"I really like you," I whisper.

"I really like you too."

I move my kisses to her inner thighs, and she moans in response.

"You're going to come one more time on this couch, and then I'm fucking the shit out of you."

"If you insist," she teases.

"I insist ... and I'm going to come fast because I'm so turned on. But then I'm going to fuck you again ... and probably a few more times."

28

Anna

"How will you know when I've recovered?" I ask as Chad's placing kiss after kiss down my leg, making me squirm and giggle.

"One more sassy comment, and I'll be buried between your legs."

I bite my lip, considering if I should make one more sassy comment or enjoy the teasing he's currently up to. "How come you still have your clothes on?"

"Because you haven't taken them off me."

"Look who's being sassy now."

He bites his lip, looking conflicted. "I'm a little nervous to take my shirt off."

"Why?" *Seriously, why?*

"I have a bad tattoo."

Immediately intrigued, I grab for his shirt. He doesn't let me, holding onto my wrists and pressing them down into the couch. Fuck is this hot.

"You're going to laugh."

"Stop building it up. Let me see it." I playfully thrash,

but I really do like him pinning me down. Releasing my wrists, Chad swoops his shirt off. "What is this?!"

"A drunken mistake."

"Chad!" My jaw is on the floor, staring at a circular tattoo that goes around his belly button. It's like a crown of thorns design. "Is this why you didn't send a shirtless gym picture?"

He nods, and outside of this tattoo being so ridiculous, I check out his thick and solid shirtless body. Chest hair. *Zaddy.*

"Do you have any other tattoos?"

"This one scared me straight."

"Why not get it removed if you don't like it?"

"It's a reminder that I can't escalate things for the story every time and that I need to grow up."

"I like that you're fun."

"Fun and immature are two different things."

I giggle, staring at it. A fucking belly button tattoo. "This made my night."

"I like that challenge."

"It wasn't—"

He leans down, pulling my thighs up and around his face. My eyes go wide feeling his nose rubbing me over my underwear. *Another first.*

"I could be down here for hours."

"Hours. Yeah right."

"You haven't picked up on the fact that I take dares seriously?" he asks between my legs before biting my underwear.

I chuckle, thinking about his belly button tattoo and him being at the bar with the bunny mask.

"Maybe you shouldn't dare me ..." he says, looking up at me from between my legs. "Unless you want to."

A giddy noise comes out of me, and he pulls my underwear down. "So sexy," he says, running his hand down my body.

"I feel sexy."

"Good. Now I want you to feel my tongue."

We smirk at each other, and I flinch when he immediately starts making circles on my clit. "Fuck," I exhale, loving the intensity.

29

Chad

I almost huff into a laugh after tasting her. Everything about her is perfect, feeding my obsession. Thinking about her fantasies, the kidnapping and murder comments she's made, I want to do something wild. I want to make this night unforgettable.

"Chad," Anna moans out. Sliding two fingers in, I make circles inside of her. "Shit," she pants.

I pull back to look at her. "I think you want to be louder."

She giggles and closes her eyes, and I go back to flicking and sucking. My mind wanders, thinking about what I can do next. I think she wants to be chased and pinned down. I think she would like that. She wants to be scared a little. We're going to have to watch scary movies, and when it gets to the part where her heart's racing, I'll have to start touching her. I want to give her everything and more. Anna Clark is everything.

Her moan pulls me back to the present. "Be loud for me." I keep my fingers busy inside of her. "Really fucking loud." She smirks, and I add, "No one will hear you." I wink, playing into her little kidnap fantasy that she so clearly craves—one I'll have to give her soon.

She closes her eyes, moaning loudly. "You sure I'm not going to murder you?" I tease, testing the waters, seeing if this dirty talk has the effect I think it will.

"Yeah," she pants.

"I don't know ..." Her eyes flick open, a hint of fear sparking in them before she giggles again. I lean back down, flicking my tongue around her a few times before asking, "Did you tell your sister where you are right now?"

"Chad," she gasps.

"Rookie mistake, not sharing your location." Our eyes lock, and I know her heart's racing in all the right ways. "There's nothing but acres of farmland around here."

"You're going to murder me?" she asks, her voice dripping with sex.

"First, I'm going to torture you."

The lip bite. Anna *fucking* Clark. Kissing her thigh, I've decided. Let's be fucking crazy.

30

Anna

"Where are you going?" I nearly yell as Chad leaves the living room without a word.

All I hear is his chuckle as he walks down the hall. I was so close, and he just left. Loudly exhaling, I wonder what's next. The last thing he said was that he's going to torture me.

What did I provoke? What is he going to do? What's he getting? He has to be getting something, right? Rope, maybe. *You're fucking deranged, and now you're about to get exactly what you asked for.* Lying on his couch, naked, the seconds tick by and my excitement grows.

"Chad!" I yell impatiently. No response, but I hear his footsteps coming back toward me.

"Oh my God." I giggle, seeing him in a bunny mask, shirtless and wearing jeans.

"You better run, little bunny," he says, leaning against the wall, staring at me.

"What?"

"Run."

I stare into the big, glassy eyes of the mask. "Run?"

"Run, little bunny," he commands again.

Run! He's going to chase me. *Fuck yes!* I hop off the couch and bolt.

31

Chad

"Outside." I chuckle, watching her run out the front door. I hadn't considered that. I thought she'd run down the hall and end up in my bedroom.

My little bunny, naked and barefoot, running outside. I bite my lip, smirking.

If she's down, we have to fuck on the grass. *Condom.* I sprint to my room, then race out the door.

32

Anna

My heart's racing as I sprint across his yard. We're really doing this! I glance back and see Buttons stepping down from the front door. Shit. I run faster. In the dark, that mask is terrifying. Giggling as I run, this is—

"Fuck!" He's fast. His hands grip my hips, and he tackles me down. I try to fight him off as best I can. "Get off me!" I yell, giggling. *Why can't I stop giggling?*

"Fuck, you're strong," he says, pinning my arms down on the cold grass.

"Buttons, no!" I giggle, staring up at him.

He chuckles behind the mask.

"Do not fuck me with that mask on!"

"You sure you don't have a thing for Buttons?"

"I've never had a thing for Buttons." I giggle as his hands possessively squeeze me.

Chad tosses the mask aside. With my one free arm, I pinch his nipple, and he wraps his hand around my neck in response.

"How are you going to murder me?"

"With my cock."

We both laugh, and he lets go of my arm but keeps his other hand lightly around my neck. Why do I love that his hand is always there? I don't fight back this time and watch as he pulls a condom from his jean pocket.

"Fuck me."

He releases my neck, pulling down his jeans and briefs just enough and slides the condom on. "I love that your crazy ass wants this."

"You said I was passionate and reasonable."

He chuckles deeply, likely remembering that's what he said when he read my palm. Shifting off me so he's still on his knees, his eyes darken with a more serious intensity.

"Get on your fucking hands and knees."

"No."

"Hands and fucking knees."

I try to hold back my smirk, but he forcefully turns me over, hiking my hips up. He bites my ass, and I whimper. *Another first.* He squeezes my cheek so hard I instinctively moan.

"Such a brat. I'm going to spank you before I fuck you to death."

I huff a challenging sound but lose my breath as the hard spank lands. My mind goes blank until I feel him enter me, fucking me hard. I finally manage a sharp inhale, feeling him deep inside. It's like I left my body for a few seconds. I'm lost in this scene, this fantasy, this man.

33

Chad

I think I spanked the sass right out of her. She's been quiet since, but the way her ass is pressing back into me says she's into this. "Tell me. Harder or stop?"

"Harder," she pants.

"Fuck, Anna."

My heart's racing, from the run and from how much I like this. I fist her hair, pressing her cheek into the grass. "So naughty, trying to escape."

Her pants have replaced the giggles. She's given in. She's letting me take her, and I'm giving her every inch. Feeling the goosebumps on her skin, I lay on top of her, smothering her with my body weight as I fuck her.

"I caught you," I whisper in her ear. "You're mine." She squirms, then moans the sexiest little noise. "This is just the beginning. I'm not letting you go." My lips stay at her ear, and I slow my thrusts. "Let me take what's mine." Grabbing her hands, I hold them behind her. "You want to be my captive. You want me to take this body."

She moans as I thrust harder, picking up the pace.

"After I've fucked you in every position, I'm going to breed you." I smirk, loving how turned on she is, how wet she is, loving every sound she makes. "I'm not afraid, but I want to have all of you first. I'm going to take my three years serious-ly." Flicking my tongue around her ear, I sharply inhale, on the edge. "I'm taking everything you'll give me."

"I'm going to come," she pants, sounding surprised.

I keep the pace steady, not changing a thing. "Come for me, little bunny. I want to feel you pulse on this cock."

Fuck. I feel her contracting around me as she screams out.

"Good girl."

I move my hands to her hips, lifting them as I rail her hard, wanting her to be so overstimulated when I come. The whines coming out of her ... "Fuck, baby." I swat her ass, thrusting deep as I come. Collapsing on top of her, I breathe heavily into her hair before rolling over onto the grass. Staring up at the stars, I catch my breath as she cuddles into me.

My fingers trail up and down her arm as I recover.

"Carry me," I hear her say, breaking me from the bliss.

"Your feet don't work anymore?"

"Nope."

I slide off the condom, tie it, and slip it into my pocket before pulling up my briefs and jeans.

"Souvenir?" Anna chides.

Standing, I look down at her. "I'm not leaving a condom in my yard." I bite my lip, admiring her naked body in the moonlight. "Piggyback ride, or do I carry you like a baby?"

"Piggyback."

I grab the bunny mask, then bend down as she hops on my back.

"That was the hottest thing ever," she says into my ear.

"It was. You're freezing, so I'm going to focus on cuddling you and warming you up when we get inside."

"Aftercare." She giggles devilishly.

"You sure you've only been vanilla?"

"My book boyfriends have taught me a lot."

34

Anna

Snuggled up in his bed, both of us naked, I feel perfect. The warmth of his body against mine, his arm draped across my waist. It's quiet, peaceful. We're comfortable just being together.

Replaying what happened over and over, my cheeks hurt from smiling.

"You said you wanted to breed me," I say into the silence.

"Too much?" He rolls onto his side, propping his head up to look at me.

"It, like, really did something to me. More than 'good girl.' But I don't want you saying it all the time—I don't want to, like, speak it into existence."

"You think that's how it works?"

"I know that's not how it works." I swat his chest. "But I should tell you, I'm not on birth control."

"Little bunny," he growls, more into this than I expected. Not the usual reaction where it's assumed it's my job to prevent pregnancy.

"Are you okay with condoms? I track my cycle, and the

odds of me getting pregnant right now are really low, even without one."

"Thank you for telling me." He leans in, tenderly kissing me. "We can skip condoms if you pee on one of those sticks with the smiley face or no smiley face beforehand."

"How do you know about ovulation tests?"

"Sisters."

"You're not freaked out that I'm not on birth control?"

"No, but if you end up getting pregnant, we're keeping the baby."

"We are?"

"Of course we are, but I want you to give me three years. After that, I'm breeding you. You're always going to be pregnant."

"I'm stopping at three kids."

"Come on, we can do four."

"Chad."

He pulls me in for a kiss.

"So, we'll use condoms during my ovulation window, and not during the other times."

"What about the other guys?"

I swat his chest, and he grabs my wrist, getting back on top of me. "There are no other guys."

The smile on his face right now as he straddles me—so smug. Of course there are no other guys.

"What do you think about wearing this bracelet every day?" he asks, playing with it on my wrist, his gaze serious.

"Will it turn my wrist green?"

"No."

"So, it's, like, expensive?"

"You're special."

"Why would I wear it every day?"

"Because ... you're my girlfriend."

"You want me to be your girlfriend?"

"Yes, but do *you* want to be my girlfriend?"

"Yes."

Chad's lips crash into mine, and I'm so excited about all of this. Chad Braun. He's exactly what I want, and he's serious about giving me everything.

"You still feel cold," he says, breaking our kiss. "Little spoon time."

I relax into his arms as he holds me tight, loving how safe and special I feel.

"How often do you wear hats?" I ask, breaking the silence.

"A lot in the summer."

I shift, turning to face him as he lies on his back, adjusting his arm so it's still around me. Resting my head on his chest, I trace little patterns along his arm. "How often do you wear your hat backwards?"

He tilts his head slightly, looking down at me. "When I'm indoors."

"Only put it backwards when you're flirting with me."

"Why?"

I bite my lip, feeling the heat rise in my cheeks. "It's hot."

He laughs quietly, his hand slipping up to play with my hair. "Yeah?"

"Yeah," I say, nodding. "It's a new turn-on for me after watching all these guys on TikTok put their hats backwards."

"And that's hot to you?"

"It could be our signal."

"Signal?"

"That I want you to pull me into a corner and fuck me."

"What else do you find so hot?"

"A lot of things."

"Like?"

I pull back enough to look him in the eyes. "Aggressive belt removal."

"Easy enough." He chuckles before kissing my forehead.

I snuggle closer to him, resting my head on his chest again, feeling the rise and fall of his breathing.

"I like this."

"Me too."

"How do you feel about cheesy holiday traditions?"

"I love them, but I'm not doing a 5K on Thanksgiving. Please tell me your family is not that kind of family."

"No. My family is the mimosa kind."

"Thank God."

"How do you feel about crypto?"

"I don't really know anything about it."

"Good."

He squeezes me before asking, "When does your lease end?"

"August."

Chad hums, and I giggle.

"I'm not moving in with you until we're engaged."

He chuckles, then kisses my temple. I smile, letting my eyes close as I relax into him. As I drift off, the only thought on my mind is how much I love being his little bunny.

35

Chad

One month later
Tuesday, May 27th

"Are you ready to meet my friends?" I ask, glancing over at Anna in my truck as we head to Jake's post Memorial Day dinner party. She looks beautiful in a short, flowy sundress and a little tan on her skin.

"Yes." She smiles over, and I grab her hand, kissing her wrist with the bunny bracelet. "Did you wear a baseball hat just for me?"

I wink at her. "Did you wear that sundress just for me?" I rake my eyes down her, admiring Anna, before returning my gaze to the road. When we pull up to Jake's house, I take a breath. "Alright, quick rundown—Jake's the firefighter I told you about. I'm not really feeling the girl he's been dating for the last month."

"Why?"

"Jake's so cool and interesting, and she ... breathes air."

"Chad," Anna scolds.

"Well, you'll see what I mean." I hesitate, consid-

Run, Little Bunny

ering the dynamics tonight. "Nicholas and Emily will be there, and so will Chris and Lauren. Chris and Lauren are going through a rough patch, and with Nicholas and Emily all happily coupled up, it might get … interesting."

"Have I been briefed enough, or can we go inside?" Anna raises a brow.

I reach over, cupping her jaw and kissing her deeply. "We don't have to stay long. I know the past few days have been crazy for you."

"I think Memorial Day was busier for you."

"Highest rental volume in the company's history."

Hand in hand, we walk to Jake's door, and everything feels perfect. She stops me with a look. "Are you going to let yourself in?"

I pause, a little surprised. "Should I knock?"

She nods, and I swat her playfully, coaxing her forward. "Get inside."

Inside, she slips off her shoes and glances around Jake's open, modern living room. "I love this house."

"More than mine?" I tease, nudging her.

"Definitely not."

"Don't let me forget. We need to talk to Jake about your lease."

"You're silly."

"I'm obsessed with you," I whisper as we walk toward the back of the house where the group is gathered.

Jake is standing at the open refrigerator. I give him a quick nod. "Jake, this is Anna."

"Unit 104," Jake says, reaching out to shake her hand. "Nice to meet you. Hope you weren't too freaked out by me giving Chad your apartment number."

"I think it worked out alright."

I laugh softly, loving her sense of humor. "So ... her lease is up in August."

"Dude, are you guys moving in together already?"

"Chad wishes." Anna giggles, glancing up at Jake. "Would it be possible to move to a month-to-month lease in August?"

"Ahh ..." Jake hesitates, looking between Anna and me. "I don't usually offer that since no one moves into apartments in the winter ... but anything for my man Chad."

I wrap my arm around Anna's shoulders. "I'll have her out of there before winter." Leaning down, I kiss her temple. "Six months is October," I whisper, and she leans into me.

"Can we help with anything?" Anna asks, and I give her waist a little squeeze, unable to resist.

Obsessed is an understatement. Our road trip and long weekend in South Haven, Michigan, two weeks ago was fucking perfect. Anna is absolutely the one. I've never been more sure of anything in my life.

I've spent every free second with her over the past month. I briefly met her sister Megan and nephew Cam a few days ago and can't wait to get to know her family better. I also can't wait for her to meet mine soon.

"Chad," Anna says, nudging me.

"What?"

"Are you going to help me with these trays?"

"Oh, sorry ... I was thinking about something." I grab the meat and cheese platter from the kitchen counter.

As we head out to the backyard, she teases, "You're going to propose to me on Halloween, aren't you?"

Smiling, I lean in. "I bet your crazy ass would love that."

She smirks. Her crazy ass *would* love that. That's the plan now. Halloween it is.

"Where's Cassy?" I ask, setting the tray on the picnic table in Jake's backyard.

"No more Cassandra."

I don't know what to say. It's not like they were serious.

"Anna," Emily's voice breaks the silence. "Sit next to me. I'd love to get to know the girl who has Chad acting like a fully formed adult."

"Ha!" I laugh. I never really knew Emily growing up but am getting to know her through Nicholas. She's great.

The girls chat for a while as I catch up with my friends.

"Another beer?" Jake asks.

"All set."

"More wine, Anna?"

Anna flashes me a look. *What's she thinking?* She stands, moving toward me.

"I'll bring a bottle from the fridge after I go to the bathroom," she says, standing behind me and turning my hat backward.

Little bunny!

Watching Anna walk inside, I can't fumble this opportunity. She wants a quickie, and she's getting one.

36

Anna

Let's see if Chad can pick up on what I'm putting down. I know I said he could signal he wants a quickie by turning his hat backward, but I want one *right* now. Glancing out the kitchen window, I smile, seeing him approach.

"Little bunny," he whispers with an intensity burning in his eyes. "Quicker than quick."

Chad squeezes my waist before tossing me over his shoulder and carrying me out of the kitchen. I nearly squeal in anticipation of the thrill. He sets me down in what looks like a guest bedroom and immediately wraps his hand around my neck, pinning me against the door.

"What's got you so turned on?" he breathes into my ear and presses kiss after kiss on my neck. His hand stays firmly in place, while the other trails up my thigh.

"This life."

"This life?"

"Yeah ... how perfect it feels."

He grumbles, dipping his fingers beneath my underwear. I flinch at the touch as he wastes no time fingering me while also stimulating my clit.

"I thought you were going to fuck me against the wall," I pant, loving the way he touches me.

"You're the horny one. You need to come."

"Need?"

"Yes. When we get home, we're doing that scene you were telling me about."

I love him.

Smiling as his lips tenderly kiss my neck and as his fingers do exactly what I want, I close my eyes, enjoying how this current fantasy is unfolding.

"Anna," he says low, and I flick open my eyes. "You're so fucking wet. I need to taste you."

Eating me out in my landlord's guest bedroom? "I don't know."

"You're afraid now?" Chad laughs, but the sex in his eyes. He wants to do it. I look over at the bed, unsure.

"I don't think that will be quick."

He grumbles in agreement as his thumb caresses my throat, moving back and forth while his eyes lock onto mine. I lean against the wall, starting to lose myself in the sensation of Chad's fingers inside me.

"What?" I ask, sensing he wants to say something.

He bites his lip, then kisses me deep. This kiss is commanding. He's taking my lips as his fingers fuck me relentlessly hard. "Come for me," he barely says, pulling back. "Silently."

Why does that turn me on even more?

"Don't you dare ..." Chad's lips move to my ear, "make one fucking sound."

"A—" His lips crash into mine, cutting me off as I teeter on the edge. I bite down on his lip hard, so close.

"You are everything," he manages to get out as I continue to bite down. Chad's grip tightens on my throat, reaching the agreed-upon limit, and I can barely breathe before I feel my contractions on his fingers.

He kisses my forehead before slipping the two fingers that were inside me into his mouth. "More of this later. Go open that wine."

I turn for the door handle, smirking and excited for later.

"One more thing," Chad says, and I look back. "I love you."

My eyes immediately well with happy tears. Memories of him in the Easter bunny costume and even before that—when he'd come into the restaurant, always fun, always bringing a smile to my face—rush through my mind. There wasn't a lack of options in town; he was under my nose the whole time.

"I love you too."

Review Page

Do you want to help the author get more recognition?

Please review this book!

Review via: Goodreads.com

Or via your purchase platform!

About The Author

Writing under the pen name, Serena Pier is a wine lover, coffee snob & wife. With Midwestern roots, her stories are primarily set in and around Chicago. Serena is deeply fascinated by power dynamics; her stories always explore unequal social status.

Thank you for reading *Run, Little Bunny: A High Five Novella*. It's the fourth in a series of five holiday themed novellas.

Check out other books in Serena Pier's Geneva Lake's Universe at www.SerenaPier.com.

Follow Serena Pier on TikTok and Instagram: @SerenaPierWrites

www.ingramcontent.com/pod-product-compliance
Ingram Content Group UK Ltd.
Pitfield, Milton Keynes, MK11 3LW, UK
UKHW022129110325
456116UK00010B/244